Mountain Chase

"I'll drop you, Billy," Raider warned. "You got three seconds to put up your paws. Otherwise you're pickin' lead out of your chest."

Raider's finger rested on the trigger of the Winchester.

Billy wasted no time. He swung around with the knife, hurling it at the big man. Raider twisted, catching the blade as it lodged in the butt of the rifle. Billy jumped toward the slopes and started to climb.

Santos drew the old Navy, trying to fire back at the big man. But the percussion caps did not spark the damp powder.

A multitude of thoughts always ran through Raider's head right before he killed a man. The half-breed scrambled between the rocks, climbing as fast as his arms and legs would carry him.

If vengeance belonged to the Lord, the big man thought, justice surely belonged to men . . .

THE GUNS OF
EL DORADO

B

BERKLEY BOOKS, NEW YORK

THE GUNS OF EL DORADO

A Berkley Book/published by arrangement with
the author

PRINTING HISTORY
Berkley edition / October 1987

ISBN: 0-425-10432-X

A BERKLEY BOOK ® ™ 757,375
Berkley Books are puublished by the Berkley Publishing Group,
200 Madison Avenue, New York, NY 10016
The name "BERKLEY" and the "B" logo
are trademarks belonging to the Berkley Publishing Corporation.

PRINTED IN THE UNITED STATES OF AMERICA

10 9 8 7 6 5 4 3 2 1

Dedicated to Jon Saxe, The Fishin' Musician

CHAPTER ONE

The Sangre de Cristo Mountains of northern New Mexico peaked high above Raider, threatening to block out the red-orange circle of an afternoon sun which balanced on the crest of the skyline. To the right and left of Raider's plodding gray gelding spread rich, summer-thickened grasslands, rolling bumps of green that ended in the thin forests at the base of the Sangre de Cristos. The big, Arkansas-born Pinkerton reined up the gray in order to study the thin wisp of wood smoke that rose out of a chimney back in the trees.

A sun-faded Stetson rode low over Raider's black eyes. His rugged, grizzled face had been darkened by the August sun, smoothing out some of the scars and wrinkles that had accumulated over the years, physical evidence of hard cases solved. A nose too many times busted but never broken, thick black hair, a bushy untrimmed mustache, his defiant jaw and proud chin set at a confident angle.

His denim pants were wet, his brown Justin boots water-logged from the storms of summer, rusting spurs at the heel. A leather vest covered a dark cotton shirt, which covered his broad chest. Everything was just a little short because Raider was bigger than most men, several inches over six feet.

He took a deep breath of fresh, moist mountain air that cooled quickly as the sun buried itself in the cairn-summit of the Sangre de Cristos.

The structure in the forest was a two-story, brown-planked house where Raider was sure he had been before. He had been in every state west of the Mississippi in his travels for Allan

1

Pinkerton and the Pinkerton National Detective Agency, so it was hard to remember some things as they had exactly happened. Why had he been in that dilapidated hole of a house? Had he been shot there? Or had he recovered from something else?

A surge of memory coursed through him. He recalled a long fall into darkness, crashing into an icy spring pool at the bottom of the cliff. Then he had woken up in the house after the fall. Or had that been in Colorado?

It did not matter.

Raider drew back the gray slicker that had kept the rain off him for five days. His hand closed around the handle of his .45-caliber Colt Peacemaker. He lifted the iron hog-leg and spun the cylinder. The six-shooter was oiled and smooth, no sign of rust. He dropped the pistol back into his holster and urged the gray forward toward the house.

Raider's gun hand hung low as he neared the porch of the dwelling. There was every reason to believe that the man he was chasing might be inside the house. Billy Santos knew the territory as well if not better than Raider. He had been born in New Mexico. That made him even more dangerous.

The New Mexico Territorial Marshal's office had lost seven good deputies trying to corral Santos. Billy had been on a spree of robbing and killing, prompting the marshal to contact the Pinkerton Agency for a man capable of apprehending the half-Mexican, half-Indian outlaw.

Raider had been impressed with the notches on Santos's belt—two trains, three stagecoaches, a wagon caravan, twelve general stores, a bank, and a Wells Fargo office. Along the way, Apache Billy (as he was called by the locals) had left behind a dozen or so dead bodies, besides those of the seven deputies. Santos believed it was better to kill the first person who gave him trouble during a holdup, because the other victims were quieter if they thought they might cash in their chips.

Raider reined back at the bare hitching post. He swung his right leg over the saddle horn and dropped to the ground with a thud. He squared his shoulders to the porch, reaching for his rifle as the door opened. Raider levered the Winchester and brought it up into the severe face of a skinny, straw-haired woman in a faded blue dress.

The woman just glared at the barrel of the rifle with narrow hawkeyes. "Don't have to shoot me. I ain't got no more money. It's all done been stole." Her voice quavered. "You can just ride on, mister."

Raider eased the bore of the rifle toward the sky, keeping it ready in case he had to use it. He knew enough not to trust the woman. But he also saw the fear in her pale blue eyes.

"Ain't lookin' to rob you." he said. "Lookin' for a man name of Billy Santos. Half-breed. Rode this way after he robbed a Wells Fargo office."

She snapped it out: "He ain't here!"

Raider studied her wrinkled face. Not as old as she looked. Eyes glassed over. Thin, weathered, trembling lips. He peered at her cracked hands. Shaking like a New Orleans blue crab freshly dropped in a kettle of boiling water. Scared to death. Of him?

Raider tilted back his Stetson. He shifted the rifle to his left side, resting it at an angle on his hip. He nodded slowly, trying to appear friendly to her.

"Go on," he urged, "tell me, ma'am. Has Billy Santos been here causin' trouble for you?"

She wiped her hands on the front of her dress. "Just get out of here. Go. Now."

Raider rested his gun hand on the butt of his Colt. "I'd like to come in, ma'am. Rest awhile. Maybe you could rustle me up somethin' to eat. I could pay you for a meal. A dollar."

"No food!" She looked back over her shoulder into the shadows of the house. When she turned back to Raider, she said, "Leave. We got sickness here. Cholera."

Raider started for the front steps.

"No!" she cried, her eyes bulging. "You can't go in there."

He stopped with his foot on the bottom step, trying to see past her into the house. "Ma'am, I got to ask you to let me look inside. Just step over there an' wait while I—"

She backed up, stretching her arms over the threshold. "Just go," she whimpered. "Please."

Raider reached into his vest pocket for his credentials. "I'm a Pinkerton, ma'am. I'm helpin' out the New Mexico marshal."

She leaned forward, her voice a rasping whisper. "Don't you understand?" she pleaded. "If you don't leave, he'll kill us. He'll—"

The twin barrels of a scattergun erupted from inside the house. The back of the woman's head disappeared right in front of Raider's black eyes. She tumbled forward down the porch steps.

A whooping cry reverberated through the air. An Apache war cry. Raider had heard it before. He dived for the ground, rolling under the porch.

Footsteps clattered above him on the planks. He looked out to see a man leaping from the porch onto the back of his gray. Apache Billy dug five-star spurs into the sides of the horse, pounding toward the mountains.

Raider rolled out and scurried to his feet. He raised the Winchester and aimed it toward the fleeing Santos. He put the silhouette in his sights and fired a single burst.

Santos grabbed his arm, flinching with pain. But he did not fall off the saddle. And he did not stop. He was out of range for the second shot from the Winchester.

"Damn!" Raider muttered under his breath.

Santos had to have a mount stashed somewhere. Raider headed for the back of the house, where he found a fresh black stallion tied to a tree. Raider had to give it to Apache Billy—he only stole the best.

The big man swung into the saddle, thinking it would be easy to catch the tired gray. It might not be as easy to catch Santos. Apache Billy was at home in the hills.

As he guided the stallion around the house, he caught sight of the half-headed woman lying at the bottom of the steps. If she had just gotten out of the way, she might have been alive. Raider decided to bury her after he found Santos. He hoped it didn't take long.

He turned the black and spurred it toward the mountains.

The sun faded as Raider found the trail that ascended into the mountains. Mists hung low in the rocks and trees, making

it impossible to tell if the figure of Apache Billy lurked anywhere overhead. At least the rain-softened ground rendered
deep tracks from the gray's hooves. The semicircular markings
stood out so well in the half-light that Raider did not have to
dismount to read them. He hoped finding Santos would be as
easy.

He kept the stallion's nose pointed up the path, plodding
cautiously through the soupy coolness of the evening.

Raider's other keen senses kicked in, augmenting his limited
vision. He could not remember hearing anything as still as the
green slopes of the Sangre de Cristos. Reining back on the
stallion, he eased out of the saddle, walking on the left side of
the horse with the rifle drawn. Nothing moved in the fog,
leastways nothing he could see or hear.

A few hundred feet up the narrow trail he found the gray
lying cold dead on the ground. The poor animal had given out
on his last run. Raider lifted his eyes to the slopes. Apache
Billy was up there somewhere, waiting. As far as Raider knew,
Billy didn't have a rifle, just the scattergun and a sidearm.
He'd have to get close to try for a shot.

The big man from Arkansas sat down on the cold flank of
the gray, considering his options. Judging by the heights of
the peaks, Apache Billy would be a fool to try to climb over
them. Of course, Billy wasn't too smart to begin with, otherwise
he would never have done all that robbing and killing in the
first place. If he did try to climb over the top, Raider's best
chance would be to see him first thing in the morning and
maybe pick him off with a rifle shot. Taking him alive no
longer seemed like the best thing. Even if he didn't climb.

Raider reached for the saddlebag on the gray. His half bottle
of whiskey was gone, taken by Santos. That really made him
angry. But he tried to work through the anger, keeping his
head in spite of everything.

What was Billy Santos most likely going to do? Given his
Apache blood, he would probably sneak around and try something tricky. In his stagecoach robberies, he had stretched out
on the ground as though he'd been left for dead by bandits.
For the bank robbery he had dressed up as a woman. And even

though Billy was a woman killer and a runner, he still hated all lawmen, which certainly qualified Raider as a possible target.

"What's he gonna do?" the big man muttered to himself, his eyes scanning the slopes. "Run or fight, Billy? What'll it be?"

Something fluttered in the mist to his left. Raider fired the Winchester twice. A mule deer scampered down the trail away from him, its tail flapping as it leapt into the trees.

Raider sighed, shaking his head, realizing that he was sweating in the cool air. He had reason to sweat. He wasn't alone on the mountain.

Two more shots rang out to match the lonely echoes of the bursts from the Winchester. Mud kicked up to his left, near the hooves of the black. Raider jumped for the neck of the stallion, wrestling it to the ground so it wouldn't be hit. After a few seconds, the animal was still.

Raider peeked over the saddle, peering into the shadows of the fog. Apache Billy's laughter rolled down the slopes through the hellish mist. Lucky, the big man thought, that he didn't have a rifle up there. He was too high for the range of the pistol or the scattergun.

"Pinkerton!" Billy cried. "I will kill you! I will tear out your heart and feed it to my brothers!"

Raider marked the direction of the voice and fired two more bursts into the mist.

Laughter again from the outlaw. "You can't hit what you don't see, white lawman. Leave me be or I will kill you."

So he was going to fight. Raider stayed low, waiting. He could fight as well. In fact, he was pretty sure he could out-trick Billy if he played it right. Billy would come sneaking in the night, trying to find Raider to slit his throat. And Raider planned to make it easy for Santos to find him. Real easy.

Billy Santos hadn't gotten the best of breaks in life. He had been born to a Mexican woman who had been raped in an Apache raid. Nobody except his mother had wanted him, and even she had been at her wit's end before she passed on. Some said that Billy's meanness had killed her. Others claimed that he had slit her throat himself, taking her few pesos to strike out to Mexico when he was barely old enough to ride.

They hadn't wanted Billy in Mexico either. Nobody seemed to want him, which was all right with Billy since his ornery streak made it difficult for him to get along with other people. He didn't want to be with anybody any more than they wanted him around.

When he showed up again in New Mexico, Billy was a grown man with no skill or trade. He had tried wrangling, but those who did hire him were quick to let him go. Outlawing had been the only viable trade for Apache Billy, and he had taken to it with a vengeance. As a man in the middle, not wanted by Indians, Mexicans, or whites, he had sought to pay back everyone for his bad fortune. They just plain had it coming, he thought.

Just like the Pinkerton who was chasing him. The big man was good, the best who'd ever come after him. But the big Pinkerton had it coming. He had to die, to even up the score for all the indignities suffered by the half-breed bandit. Billy knew he had to be careful, though, because the tall lawman was pretty clever himself. His one rifle shot had nicked Billy's arm.

Santos had to marvel at the way Raider had found him. He had chased him over ground that left no tracks, obviously picking up on the dung and urine left behind by the mount. Santos had heard how good Pinks were at tracking, but he had never believed it until Raider was on his tail.

So the half-breed outlaw had waited through the night, watching as the Pinkerton built a fire below. He dozed in the misty air, waking a few hours before dawn to see that the fire had died. It was then that Apache Billy took out his knife and started down toward Raider's camp.

A light wind began to stir the mist and leaves as Billy descended. It seemed almost a shame to kill such a worthy adversary. The big Pinkerton was making it too easy, just lying there by the last coals of the fire, the black stallion tied far enough away that he wouldn't wake even if the animal spooked.

Billy paused at various intervals along the way, watching the prone body to make sure Raider hadn't heard him.

The tall man's body was stretched out, boots still on, the faded Stetson covering his head, which rested on the saddle.

The grinning outlaw hunkered on a rock, thinking that the tall man would never hear him coming with his moccasined feet. For a second, Santos considered just shooting him from above, a well-placed volley from the pistol to chop up Raider's head. No, he decided, he wanted the pleasure of slitting his throat, opening up a bloody smile from ear to ear, paying him back for the stung arm.

He started down again, quieter than a sidewinder breaking across a sandy dune. His arm didn't really hurt that much; it just made him madder.

Billy's criminal mind relished the thought of conquest. He pictured the image of Raider's crimson throat over and over in his head. He wasn't sure who he would tell about the incident, but he'd find somebody to brag to sooner or later.

Green leaves and mossy rocks held droplets of dew as Santos slithered closer to the sleeping body. He thought he heard snoring, which was good enough to mask his arrival. His thumb felt the edge of the moist blade.

Billy decided to come in the front way, toward Raider's head. He could reach down over the saddle, lift the head, and open him up with a quick stroke. Then he'd mount the black and light out for Mexico again. At least he could speak the Spanish his mother had taught him. There wasn't much law in Mexico, either. All he had to do was stay away from the *federales*. Hell, they didn't care if you robbed a few peasants, raped their sisters and daughters, killed a farmer or two.

His feet fell softly on the trail.

He saw the Stetson on the saddle.

Billy loved the easy kill. After the Pinkerton was gone, he'd strip the body, steal his money, his guns, even the thick blanket that covered his long frame. Easy.

Santos's brown eyes were wide as he approached the saddle. His chest heaved up and down. No man gets used to killing, in spite of how he may love or hate the act. His body reacts to the impending death of another.

He reached down for the Stetson, his hand dropping slowly.

A handful of hair. The blade sweeping in one fatal motion. He expected to lift a head, but the hat came up with a hunk of black hair from the stallion's tail. Santos kicked the blanket. Twigs and leaves fell out.

"Mornin', Billy. Nice of you to come by like this."

Santos spun back toward the deep voice. Raider held the Winchester dead level with his heart. The outlaw's face was agape.

"Easy, boy," Raider said, eyeing the blade of the knife. "Just drop that hog sticker and put your hands toward the sky."

Santos was frozen, the coyote caught over the prey in the bright light of a reflecting lantern.

Raider peered down the barrel of the Winchester. "Hands up, Billy."

Santos had the look in his eyes, like he was thinking about another run. His gun hand wasn't far from the old Navy Colt at his side. The knife was still in his fingers.

"I'll drop you, Billy," Raider warned. "You got three seconds to put up your paws. Otherwise you're pickin' lead out of your chest."

Raider's finger rested on the trigger of the Winchester.

Billy wasted no time. He swung around with the knife, hurling it at the big man. Raider twisted, catching the blade as it lodged in the butt of the rifle. Billy jumped toward the slopes and started to climb.

The sun was coming up good, burning off the mists. Raider could see Billy easily. Santos drew the old navy, trying to fire back at the big man, but the percussion caps did not spark the damp powder.

Raider considered chasing him, trying to talk him into giving up and coming back to Albuquerque for hanging.

Santos scrambled higher, clawing for purchase, his cries like an animal caught in a trap.

"Stop it, Billy," Raider called halfheartedly.

But he didn't stop. And Raider didn't feel like chasing him anymore. The trail had been too long already.

The big Pinkerton raised the rifle, putting Santos in his sights. He drew down between Apache Billy's shoulder blades, compensating for the slight pull to the left. It paid to know the rifle.

A multitude of thoughts always ran through Raider's head right before he killed a man. He wondered how the higher powers above would treat him come Judgment Day. How would he word his report to Allan Pinkerton? Would the territorial government give him a ration of shit for not bringing Santos back alive?

The half-breed scrambled between the rocks, climbing as fast as his arms and legs would carry him.

Raider remembered the half-headed woman who had died in a twin-barreled burst from Apache Billy's scattergun.

If vengeance belonged to the Lord, the big man thought, justice surely belonged to men.

He squeezed off a single round that exploded toward the fleeing madman.

Apache Billy stiffened when the round entered his body. He stumbled backward, reaching for a hidden derringer. He never got it out of his pocket. He rolled down the side of the mountain, landing a few feet away from Raider.

The big man walked closer and stood over the trembling outlaw.

Santos peered up at him with fear in his eyes. "Cold. I'm cold inside. Help me."

Raider's black eyes narrowed. "Help you? Like you helped that woman back there? Like you were gonna help me until I tricked you?"

Santos quivered, his head lolling to one side. "Cold."

"They say the fires of Hell are hot, Billy. I reckon you're gonna find out, ain't you?"

Raider turned away, walking back toward the stallion. His ears pricked as he heard the sliding of metal on cloth. A hammer clicked back. Raider spun with his rifle, delivering a single shot to Santos's forehead. Apache Billy's hand, which was full of the derringer, dropped down. Blood gushed from the hole in his brow.

Raider exhaled, his breath fogging the air. "Shoulda raised your hands when I told you, Billy."

The only thing Raider regretted was cheating the hangman.

Billy would have been the scared kind, one of those gallows boys who screamed and hollered all the way. He hadn't lived like a man, and he wouldn't have died like one.

Raider wondered if the half bottle of whiskey was somewhere in the slopes above. He finally figured that Santos had used it on his wounded arm and then had drunk the rest. Good whiskey gone to waste.

The big man strode over to his saddle. He lifted the blanket from the branches and leaves he had used to make a bogus sleeping body. Apache Billy had been stupid to fall for one of the oldest tricks in the world. Raider shook the bugs from the blanket and then pulled on his Justin boots.

He saddled the black and fixed his saddlebags in place. He'd ride the black until he found the rightful owner—if he ever found him. When the mount was ready, he looked back at Santos's body.

It would be easier just to leave him for the buzzards. That was all Santos deserved. But if he didn't get the body back to Albuquerque, the territorial marshal might raise a squawk about whether or not Raider had truly brought Santos to justice.

The big man didn't feel like arguing, so he raised the body and threw it over the saddle. He could walk for a while, at least until he found another horse or rigged an Indian travois. Santos was liable to be as much trouble dead as alive.

Raider stretched toward the sky, which was beginning to burn with the summer heat of the day. He was exhausted, as he had not slept through the night during his wait for Santos. Billy had come later than Raider had figured. The big man wanted to lie in a bed and then wake up next to a willing woman.

Woman. He thought about her, lying on the porch with her head half gone. Raider wondered what kind of man had it in him to shoot a woman. He turned and gave a little tap to the lifeless form of Billy Santos. He almost wished he could bring him back to life just to shoot him again.

Crazy thoughts, the big man figured. His head spun from lack of sleep and nourishment. He couldn't remember the last time he had eaten. It didn't make much difference. With the rumblings from his stomach, he doubted he could hold down a meal. Killing a man—even one who needed it—always told in his gut, the nervous, jittery pain that took a few hours, sometimes days to leave.

Raider grabbed the reins of the black. "Come on, boy. Let's get the hell outta here."

He walked past the decaying body of the gray. Buzzards had already gathered overhead. As soon as Raider was gone, they'd land on the carcass, tearing at it with their relentless beaks. Raider tried not to think too much about his own dying, but when he did, he offered one silent prayer—to be buried deep, where the carrion critters could not get at him. He hoped for a high, rocky cairn to keep out the coyotes and vultures. Was that too much for a man to ask for?

Raider walked the horse for a long time, keeping his eyes open. He couldn't recall how far he had come from the house. He kept looking ahead toward the sky, expecting to see buzzards over the brown dwelling. As soon as the smell reached them, the snake-necked creatures would be swarming on the woman's corpse, just as they were attacking the gray.

Billy Santos would have attracted his own sky-bound funeral procession had it not been for the living presence of Raider and the stallion.

When Raider emerged from the trees, he saw the house in the distance. His eyes widened. No buzzards. He drew his rifle, wondering why the scavengers had not yet arrived.

He kept walking, slowly, searching for the body of the half-headed woman. But he did not see her, nor did he detect the weird smell that accompanies recent death. And when he neared the foot of the steps where the woman had fallen, Raider saw that her body was gone.

CHAPTER TWO

Raider reached for the rifle scabbard on his saddle. Easing out the Winchester, he quietly levered the weapon, locking a round in the chamber. The house was quiet, at least from the outside. The front door had been closed, and the smokestack was lifeless on the planked roof.

Where had that damned body gone?

No scavenger, not even a bear, would drag away a whole human carcass. The vultures would pick it clean on the spot. A mountain lion or a coyote—even a pack of coyotes—would have done the same thing.

Raider started slowly toward the porch.

Maybe there were other people in the house. But who? Did the dead lady have any kin? Or did Billy Santos have three or four cutthroats in there, waiting for him to come back with a Pinkerton's scalp on his belt? Santos might have run to lead Raider away, thinking he could kill him and get back to his men. Had the marshal said anything about a gang?

No horses out front. Raider decided to lead the stallion around to the back. The big man cut a wide, careful circle through the thin trees. When he had the angle right, he could see that there were no horses in the back either.

Raider untied the dead man's body and luffed him off onto the ground. He guided the stallion to the back wall, climbing onto the saddle so he was high enough to peer into the dim recesses of the kitchen.

No sign of movement. Everything looked bare, as if nothing

had been touched since the last time the kitchen was cleaned. Raider drew his Colt and broke the smoked glass, reaching inside to unlatch the casement. When the window was open, the big man slipped through, landing on the kitchen floor with a cat's touch.

Raider hesitated in the stillness of the morning, listening for sounds of movement. There was nothing but the creaking boards beneath his feet. He lifted the Peacemaker and started through the house, expecting at any moment to trip over the fallen body of the half-headed woman.

By now, anyone in the house had heard him. He pushed into a room that served as an eating place and a store counter. The rickety way station was a middle ground between the plains and the mountains, a sanctuary for prospectors and drifters. Anyone could have shown up while he was off chasing Santos.

"Okay," he called, "anybody here better come on out and tell me what you done with the body of that woman."

No reply.

Maybe the person who had taken the body had come through, buried the woman, and then gone on.

Raider made sure. He searched the rest of the house but found no one. The bedrooms upstairs were deserted, both of them. He planned to utilize one of the beds as soon as he got Billy Santos into the shade. Under the porch would be best. Raider would throw something on top of him until he finished sleeping.

He went back through the house, unlatching the kitchen door. As he pushed out, he lowered his gun into the holster. Nothing to worry about. If anybody came back, he'd thank them for burying the woman.

Anyway, wouldn't there be a fresh grave nearby? As soon as he got Santos cooled down, he'd take a look. It wouldn't be hard to find.

As he turned, he saw it. His gut wrenched up like he had swallowed a bucket of lye. He could not tear his eyes away from the dangling spectacle, even though it sickened him to see it.

Hanging from the clothesline in back of the house was the

severed head of Billy Santos, gaping blindly with a horrific death-mask expression on the bloody face.

Raider heard a scream above him.

From the roof of the house came a flying body, a boyish shape that landed on the big man's shoulders. Raider saw the flashing of a knife blade as it swung around his head. The big man instinctively dropped to one knee, tossing his attacker over his shoulder, hurling him through the air.

A guttural sound escaped from the ambusher's lips. Raider hovered over him, peering down at the blade that was lodged in the stomach of a boy who was barely into his teens. The lad gasped and died with a bloody bubble on his pink lips. Raider hadn't meant to kill him. He had landed on the damned knife.

Raider felt sort of weak at the knees. "What the hell? Where did you come from, boy? Couldn't you tell who I was?"

But dead men, no matter how young or old, do not give answers.

Raider lifted him up, carrying him toward the house. Another corpse to bury. He didn't even know a thing about the kid. Maybe he had just gone crazy after Santos had come.

The big man looked back toward the head that hung on the clothesline. Maybe it was best to just bury both of them and let the marshal take his word on it. In any case, he had to find a shovel.

When the two graves were covered with dirt and rocks, it occurred to Raider to look for the third grave, that of the unfortunate woman killed by Apache Billy's shotgun blast.

He searched through the woods, finally emerging on the knoll of a meadow at the edge of the forest. His hand lifted the Colt. He saw a lone figure sitting by the ridge of a fresh grave. As he approached, he saw that the figure was a young woman.

She looked up at Raider when his shadow fell across the grave. Her hair was long and brown, her eyes dark in the sun. The dress she wore was of new calico cloth.

"My sister," she said softly.

Raider knelt down beside her. "I'm sorry. Maybe you ought to come back to the house."

She gestured back toward the house. "Did you find my cousin?"

Raider looked away. "The boy."

"Yes. I fear for his life. He's mad, you know." Her tone was simple, almost friendly in defeat. "I never wanted to come out here. I said it wasn't a good idea. And after my sister's husband was killed, I wanted to leave. But Rina, my sister, wanted to stay. She thought a new man would come along."

Raider nodded. A new man had come along. Only it was Billy Santos.

He put his hand on the woman's shoulder. She was younger than the dead sister. Her face was ash white, and she wore the hardship of the territory in her expression.

"I caught the man who did this," Raider said. "He's paid for it."

She did not seem to hear him. "Lafe, my cousin, he said we had to bury her before that Billy came back. He was going to wait on the roof and kill that Billy with a knife."

Raider sighed. "Well, your cousin met with a little accident. He fell off the roof and stabbed himself to death."

The girl began to cry uncontrollably. Raider took her close to him, reminding himself that he was giving comfort in her time of need, nothing else. He'd have to get her back to the house and then decide what to do with her. He had a bunch of questions to ask her. Did she have any kin? Did Santos do anything to her? Where did she want to go?

He lifted her to her feet and urged her back toward the wooden house.

The woman seemed to snap out of it after they got back to the kitchen. She stopped crying, and while she did not speak to Raider or even look at him, she did take to preparing a huge meal for the big man. After she fired the wooden stove, she fussed over pots and pans and then served him a piece of tender meat, mashed potatoes, wild scallions, biscuits, and gravy.

Raider ate everything she put in front of him, pausing with

his knife and fork only long enough to nod his appreciation to the brown-eyed girl.

She sat down and wiped her hands on a towel. "My name is Mindy."

"Pleased to meet you." He gestured toward the stove. "Ain't you gonna eat, Mindy?"

She shook her head, the first real response he had gotten out of her. "I ain't hungry just now." A weak smile appeared on her thin lips. "My momma never ate with the rest of us. She'd always sit by herself later, after we had all eaten."

Raider dipped a homemade biscuit into the rich gravy. "Where do you and your people hail from?"

Mindy's delicate hand pointed east. "Louisiana, in the north, near the border. Had a cotton farm till my daddy died. The place killed my husband, too. You ever cotton farm, mister?"

Raider swallowed and shook his head. "No, ma'am. Name's Raider."

For the first time she really looked at him. "Raider? What kind of name is that?"

He paused, the fork halfway to his lips. He put the fork down and smiled. "I reckon it's a name for a man who's always in trouble."

She laughed, loudly and for a long time. The laughter turned into tears, and she cried even longer. Raider felt sort of helpless just sitting there, but he didn't reach toward her. Instead, he tried to pay her a compliment by cleaning his plate.

"I'm sorry," she said finally. "There's just been so much. So much. I lost a baby out here. A little girl. She's buried up by my sister."

Raider sighed. "You just go on and cry, Mindy. Anybody's suffered as much as you today has plenty to cry about."

She stopped crying as soon as he said it and started to clean the table. Raider stood up from the table, stretching. He reached for his rifle, which was leaning against the wall. He also picked up a cloth sack that was lying next to the Winchester.

Mindy brushed a lock of brown hair away from her high forehead. "What's in that sack?" she asked, eyeing the blue cloth.

"Evidence," the big man replied.

Her lower lip trembled, and her eyes were suddenly afraid. "You leaving?"

Raider smiled. "No. I'm just goin' upstairs to rest awhile, if it's tolerable with you."

"It's tolerable." She looked down at the floor. "I don't want to stay here, Raider. I hate this place. I just want to go." Her brown eyes flashed up at him. "Anywhere."

"We'll hash it out after I've had me some sleep," he replied.

She turned back toward the wooden bucket she was using to wash the dirty dishes.

"Mindy, you all right?"

She nodded. That seemed to be enough for the big man. He started upstairs to one of the bedrooms. He thought a bed would feel good, since he hadn't been in one for a month of Sundays.

But when he stretched out, Raider found that he couldn't close his eyes. His body was tired, but his head was working overtime. The case of Billy Santos coursed through his mind from beginning to end. He considered his report to the Pinkerton Agency, what he would tell, what he would leave out. Titus Tilden, Wagner's assistant, could be damned finicky about Raider's reports. But hell, what did they want him to do? Catch outlaws, or write stories?

That bastard Tilden would have had Raider's scalp if he could have gotten a knife on it. But the big man from Arkansas knew better. Who did they always come to for the most dangerous work? They complained about the bodies he left in his wake, but who always got the telegram directing him to a chicken-picking job that nobody else wanted? Raider was the agency's ace in the hole, the fifth card to the flush. If things got rough, he was the ramrod, the troubleshooter tossed straight into the fire.

Raider sat up on the edge of the bed, full of energy when he should have been dog tired. But instead of brooding on thoughts best left alone, he decided to clean his guns. It took him the better part of the morning and half the afternoon as he serviced the Winchester and the Peacemaker, removing every speck of dirt and rust.

After he had finished, he stretched out again, this time falling into a fitful doze. He dreamed he was chasing Billy Santos again, only in the nightmare he didn't win. The outlaw's dream-shape fired the triumphant shot. When Raider felt the slug tearing into his body, he cried out and sat up, his face sweating in the coolness of the dark night.

"There, there, don't worry. It's all right. You're awake. It was only a dream."

Raider's body was shaking. He wrapped his arms around the warmth of the woman's shoulders. He hugged her, kissing her neck. She stroked the back of his head with both hands.

Raider suddenly realized what he was doing. He pushed away, holding the woman at arm's length. She wore a thick flannel nightgown. Her brown hair was down, falling on her shoulders.

"What are you doin' in here?" Raider asked.

She touched his hand on her arm. "I heard you calling out in your sleep. Having a nightmare, I'd say." She put her hand on his forehead. "You aren't sick, are you? You don't seem to have a fever."

Raider shrugged away. "No, I don't have a fever. I just need some more shut-eye. If you'll leave me be, I'll go back to sleep."

Her face changed from a benevolent smile to an unhappy frown. She started to cry again. Raider hesitated but then took her in his arms. She cried with her face on his chest. Every time he tried to push her away, she clung tighter. Raider liked her being so close to him, but it still didn't seem like the time or place.

"You better go back to your own room," he said finally.

She looked up into his eyes, tears streaming down both sides of her face. "Let me stay in here with you."

He shook his head. "Wouldn't be right."

"Who would know?" she asked. "My sister in her grave? My cousin who got himself killed?"

She had a point there.

But Raider still didn't feel right. "You seem like a proper kind of woman, Mindy. Right now you ain't in such good shape because you done lost all your kin. You don't want to do somethin' you might regret later on."

She gripped his arms. "There are ways to keep from getting a baby. My husband and I used to do it. He'd just pull out—"

"Hush that!"

Raider wasn't offended. He was excited. He had been so long without a woman that just hearing about it made him want to pull her between the sheets.

Mindy put her head against his shoulder. "My husband has been dead for two years. And just because you're a widow it don't make you stop wanting a man. You don't stop living just because your husband does. And I don't care about a thing right now. There's nobody out here but you and me, and I think it would be nice if we—"

Raider kissed her. He pressed his lips to her mouth, prompting her tongue to dart in and out. The kiss was all he had planned to do—until he felt her warmth against his trail-hardened body. Then there was no way to turn back.

Raider broke away and stood up.

Mindy grimaced. "Don't leave me."

He shook his head. "I ain't. I just want to do one thing first."

He picked up the blue sack and tossed it out the window.

"Why'd you do that?" she asked.

He took off his vest and started to unbutton his shirt. "Never mind. It ain't important."

Her bosom rose and fell as he took off his clothes. She lifted the nightgown over her head. Raider sat down next to her on the bed. When he touched her shoulder, he felt the chill-bumps on her smooth skin.

Her hand strayed over the mats of hair on his chest. "My husband had hair like this. He was my only man. Now you're gonna be my second. And it don't bother me that we ain't married."

He kissed her forehead. "You're gonna be all right, Mindy."

She found his lips again. They embraced, sitting on the edge of the bed. Raider could be tender when he wanted to, and he figured the poor woman in his arms needed it. He kissed her for a long time before he eased her down onto the feather mattress.

"I'm not afraid," she said. "I don't think there's any fear

left in me. Not after what I seen out here.''

Raider lowered his mouth to the tight nipples of her smallish breasts. Her body stiffened. He touched the sensitive places of her thighs, stroking gently toward her wedge of pubic hair.

She parted her legs for him. Raider felt her moistness on his fingertips. He slid between her lips, massaging the special places inside her.

Mindy's body relaxed. Her breathing became irregular. She threw her head back and moaned with each careful flick of his hand.

Raider felt her body shivering under his touch. He wondered if her husband had ever done *that* to her. He took her soft hand and guided it to the rigid protrusion between his muscular thighs.

A short breath escaped from Mindy's lips. ''My husband didn't have anything this big,'' she whispered.

Her hand went up and down, her palm and fingers stroking the hard length of his penis. Raider felt a rise coming out of nowhere. His body shook as the head of his prick erupted with a thick, hot stream.

Mindy laughed. ''My husband never did that, neither.''

''I been a little edgy,'' Raider replied.

She asked him if he would get soft.

He didn't.

He rolled over, positioning himself between her legs.

''Here,'' she said, ''let me wipe it off. I don't want another baby.''

She used the sheet.

When she was finished, Raider rested his cock against her cunt. She took him in her hand, guiding the prickhead between her lips. Raider eased into her, giving her a chance to adjust to his size.

For a few seconds, he just lay there inside her, relishing the warmth of her femininity. Finally, Mindy began to move underneath him, squirming, thrusting her hips upward. Raider responded by driving his hips downward, meeting her thrusts, bouncing her off the rope-spring bed.

Mindy shook her head back and forth, crying out with each rise and fall of Raider's hips. At one point she buckled, her body rocked with spasms. She grabbed Raider's shoulders, keeping him still, holding him deep inside with the contractions of her cunt.

"Don't move," she whispered. "Just don't move."

But after a while, Raider had to move. He picked up the same rhythm and Mindy did not stop to complain. Again the cornshuck mattress shook, and the floorboards beneath them threatened to give way.

The big man felt his sap rising. He grabbed the sides of the bed, using the leverage to hasten his motion. Mindy came again, shaking with the same violent release.

As her vagina tightened, Raider drove his cock to the hilt, anticipating another climax.

"Not inside," Mindy cried. "Not inside me."

Raider obliged her, pulling out at the last minute. Her hand gripped the head of his cock, jerking as he deposited a milky puddle on her stomach. Raider collapsed on top of her, kissing her cheeks and forehead.

Mindy quickly wriggled out from under him.

The big man lay back on the bed, his eyes half closed. "Where are you goin', honey?"

She pulled her nightgown on. "Back to my own bed."

"But . . ."

"I can't sleep in here," she replied. "I thought I could, but I can't now that we done it."

Raider shrugged. "Suit yourself. You're welcome to stay if you want. I ain't gonna complain either way."

She started for the door, spinning back toward him at the threshold. "You're a good man, Mr. Raider. I just want you to know that."

She turned and left.

The big man wasn't sure how good he was. Bedding the poor woman might have been the worst thing for her. He shook his head, wondering if he had let his cock get him into another bad situation. What if she went crazy again, like her cousin?

He fell asleep thinking about it. This time he didn't dream. He didn't awaken until Mindy crawled back into bed with him about dawn. The sun was well up in the sky by the time she left him again.

• • •

Raider finished reading the report he had written for Pinkerton, Wagner, and Tilden. It was a simple, concise paragraph of only two sentences. The big man had fretted more over the spelling than he had over taking the life of Billy Santos. He held it out to read it one more time.

"I, Raider, was sent by the marshal of New Mexico to find Billy Santos who has been robbing and killing all over this territorie. He would not come back of his own free will so I kilt him and buriet his body."

He signed his name.

Raider looked up from the table, watching the silent Mindy as she scraped the breakfast dishes. She had fed him the last of the eggs and salt pork, along with another tin of biscuits. She wasn't saying much after their time in bed. Was she ashamed? Raider actually felt kind of good about the whole thing. It had made him more relaxed.

"Mindy," he said, "can you read?"

She nodded.

He held out the report to her. "Will you read this?"

She took the report from him and gave it a quick glance. " 'Territory' is spelled with a 'y' on the end. 'Kilt' should be 'killed' and 'buried' has a 'd' on the end." She gave it back to him.

Raider made the corrections and asked her to read it again. She refused. He got up and moved close to her. She would not face him, but rather looked out the window into the forest.

Raider put his hands on her shoulders. "You ain't got to feel bad about last night. You didn't do nothin' wrong."

"It ain't last night that's bothering me," she replied.

Raider spun her around, peering into her brown eyes. "Then what's wrong? You can tell me, honey."

She lowered her eyes. "It's now that's bothering me. What's gonna happen to me? I can't stay here by myself."

"No, you can't."

"You're just gonna leave me, ain't you?"

Raider moved away from her, sitting at the table. "I been thinkin' about that. It's been on my mind."

She threw the dishtowel to the floor. "Then just go. Leave

me here for the prospectors and the thieves.''

Raider motioned toward the chair on the other side of the table. ''Sit down, Mindy. Go on.''

She plopped down like an angry child about to be disciplined.

''All right,'' Raider said. ''You been tellin' me what I oughta do. Now how's about tellin' me what you want.''

She fidgeted, thinking about it, almost as lost as he was for a solution. ''I don't know,'' she said finally. ''I just want to be away from here.''

''You got any kin?'' he asked.

She shrugged. ''None that I know of, alive anyway.''

''Then I'm takin' you to Albuquerque,'' he replied. ''Unless you figure on somethin' else.''

Her eyes grew wide, and she smiled, ''Really? I always wanted to go to Albuquerque.''

''We're gonna need another horse,'' Raider continued. ''You know of one hereabouts?''

She stood up, excited about the prospect of a fresh start. ''No, but there's an old buggy in a shed up the road a piece, back in the hollow.''

Raider rubbed his chin. ''I reckon that black could pull a buggy. Might be a little ornery at first, but he'll catch on.''

''Oh, Raider.''

She sat on his lap and kissed him. They almost got started again, but Raider told her to save it. They'd need their strength for the trail.

By noon the buggy was hitched up and ready to go. Raider loaded some of Mindy's belongings, along with his own gear. She took her place on the buggy seat, peering out over the trail with new confidence.

Raider climbed up beside her, swinging the blue cloth sack under the seat. It made a weighty noise when it hit, like a ripe melon. The big man made sure the bag was secure.

Mindy's brow wrinkled. ''What the devil is that thing?''

''Like I told you, honey, it's only evidence.''

He grabbed the reins and urged the black forward. The stallion skittered a little, but after a while he was fine. Raider took it slow to avoid a broken wheel on the rusty buggy.

Mindy leaned over and rested her head against his shoulder.

"I'm going to Albuquerque. Thank God."

Raider wondered if she was planning to stay with him. Sometimes women would imagine things, thinking they were going to happen when there really wasn't a prayer of it coming true. He'd keep her off him, he decided. No more loving on the trail.

But Mindy had other ideas. The first night they camped, she climbed into his bedroll, eagerly replaying their first night together. Raider was just as willing, even though he couldn't help but feel he was complicating things for himself.

When they were finished, he expected Mindy to climb back into her own bedroll. But she stayed with him the whole night, sparking a warmth that kept him comfortable until morning.

They shared the same bedroll for more than a week, until they reached the smooth dirt road that began the slow ascent into Albuquerque.

CHAPTER THREE

Raider and the woman rode into Albuquerque without attracting too much undo attention. A few gentlemen turned to look at Mindy, but they did not tip their hats when they saw the huge, grizzled man sitting next to her. The town was caught in a sleepy summer afternoon, with several of the shops boasting signs that declared, "Gone Fishing."

Naturally, the marshal's office was open for business as usual.

When the big man reined the black in front of the wooden sidewalk, he realized how much he had left to wrap up. Besides the usual work that came with ending a case, he still had to do something about the woman. He couldn't just leave her on her own.

Mindy sat wide-eyed on the seat of the buggy, taking in the window of a dress shop. "I have five dollars," she declared, "hidden in my—"

"Don't announce it to everyone," Raider said.

She started to get down.

Raider grabbed her arm. "Steady there, girl. I want you to come in with me to see the marshal."

"But why?"

"Because you may have to back up some of the things I say."

He swung out of the seat and went around to help her down. When Mindy was safely on the sidewalk, he reached beneath the seat and took out the blue cloth sack. Red stains had seeped through the bag during the trip.

Mindy grimaced. "That thing stinks."

"I put lye on it," Raider replied. "I found some behind the counter at your old place." He urged her toward the door. "Come on, first things first. Let's get it over with."

Three deputies stood up when they saw the pretty brunette striding into the office. Their hands fell toward their guns as Raider slipped in behind her. He lifted his palms to the air, stopping them from drawing down.

"Hold it, boys," he said, easing forward. "Don't y'all recognize me? Raider, remember?"

A weak-faced deputy shook his head. "That's the Pink we sent out lookin' for Billy Santos."

Raider tossed the stained sack at their feet. It bounced and rolled to a halt against the wall. All of them stepped back away from the bag.

"Better get the marshal," said the weak-faced man.

In less than five minutes the marshal was fetched from breakfast. He eyed the big man from Arkansas as soon as he entered the office. The marshal had dealt with Raider before, always with the desirable result.

"Said you brung in Santos," the marshal said. "Don't see him."

Raider pointed at the bag in the corner. "That's what's left of him."

Mindy grimaced and turned away.

The marshal nodded toward the young lady. "Who's she?"

Raider put his arm around Mindy's shoulder. "She's one of them who Santos done wrong. Killed all her kin."

Mindy looked up, crying. "That's right."

Raider pointed again toward the bag. "When I brung Santos back over a saddle, her cousin sliced off his head and hung it up to dry. There was more dead at the house, so I buried all of them. Since Apache Billy's head was already off, I figured to just bring it on in. Easier'n foolin' with the whole body."

The marshal eyed the bag, which still lay untouched in the corner. "How do I know there's a head in there?"

"Have a look," the big man replied with a grin.

The marshal turned back to Mindy. "Where's your cousin what cut off his head?"

"He up and killed himself," she replied.

Which was very close to the truth.

The marshal sighed. "Ah, damn it, Raider, we always have the same problem when you finish up some of our business."

"I ain't failed you yet," Raider said, smiling.

As the marshal pivoted and started for the blue sack, the other deputies parted to get out of his way. The chief law officer in the territory studied the bag, and for a moment Raider thought he might pick it up. But instead the marshal wheeled around, nodding his head.

"If Raider says he caught Billy Santos, then he more'n likely caught him," the marshal declared. "This case is closed."

Raider leaned in toward the lawman. "Marshal, is there any kind of reward on this thing?"

The marshal raised a bushy eyebrow. "Can't say there is. Took the reward off when I brung you on. The usual fee, wasn't it?"

Raider nodded. "Yeah, that ain't what I mean. I don't want it for myself, it's just that this little lady here ain't rightly got much to her name after her kin was killed."

The marshal's cold eyes fell on the pretty woman. "Hmm. That's a dad-burned shame."

Mindy blushed. "Why, Marshal, your language."

The aging gentleman took off his hat. "Excuse me, miss."

"I'm a widow," Mindy replied. "You can call me Mrs. Brown. Mrs. Amanda Brown. My friends call me Mindy for short."

"Can you read and write and cipher, Mrs. Brown?" the marshal asked.

"Why, yes, I can," she replied.

The marshal motioned for Raider to follow him. "I think maybe I can do somethin' for you after all. Raider, if you can spare me a minute."

They spoke in private until the big man came back to Mindy, smiling and winking at her. "All set," he said. "I'll tell you when we're outside."

"Thank you."

"Raider."

He turned back to see the marshal pointing at the blue sack, which still lay on the floor.

"Better take that with you," the marshal said. "Don't leave that head lyin' in this office."

Raider politely scooped up the sack and then led Mindy outside to the buggy.

She stepped away from him, grimacing at the sack. "Did you really bring that head back with you?"

Raider opened the sack and reached inside. "See for yourself."

He lifted something round from the bag.

Mindy shied at first, but when she saw what he was holding, she laughed and took a playful poke at him.

"Just a muskmelon," he said, a devilish expression on his face. "You can find 'em anywhere this time of year."

"Why'd'you do that?"

Raider shrugged. "Well, I didn't feel like luggin' that body all the way back here, so I figured to fool the marshal a little so he wouldn't give me a hard time. No harm done. After all, I did stop Santos."

She nodded. "I guess you did."

Raider took her arm. "Come on, honey, let's go see your new home."

Someone was trying out the new bell on the schoolhouse. It was loud and echoed through the streets, a reminder to the children of Albuquerque that summer would one day be over. Raider stood next to Mrs. Amanda Brown, who frowned at the tolling bell.

"A schoolteacher?" she remarked with uncertainty. "I don't know, Raider. It might be too difficult for me."

Raider exhaled. "Well, the marshal says their schoolteacher done got married and had herself a baby. Said she don't want to teach no more. Her husband wants to move back east, so they won't be around after September. She could help you out until then."

Mindy put a finger to her lips. "I don't know."

"What is there to it?" Raider offered. "You can read. Hell, you corrected my report. You can cipher, can't you?"

"Yes."

He threw out his hands. "Then just teach the little brats what you know. Hell, you must be smarter'n kids who are younger than you.''

She smiled. "Stay with me.''

Raider blushed, lowering his eyes. "I knew that was comin'.''

"Then you are going to leave me!'' she cried. "That's not fair.''

Raider spun back, pointing his Stetson at her. "Now you look here, woman. I never promised nothin'. You come to me in that bed. And it was loco out there for both of us. You lost your kin, and I can understand how you're grievin', but when I found you in that house, you didn't have a thing.'' He pointed toward the school. "And I think you better not pass up a chance like this. The wheel of fortune spins both ways. I know, I played it a lot in my time. Savvy?''

He thought she might cry, but instead she took her medicine, nodding in approval. "You're right. I should thank you.'' she looked up with those brown eyes. "Thank you.''

He shook his head. "Aw, don't worry about it. I just sounded off 'cause you weren't gettin' the drift.''

She put her soft hand on his cheek. "You're right about something else, too. I came to your bed. And I want to go there again before you leave. Can we do it again?''

It hurt the big man to say it. "No.''

"Why not? I don't care. And I won't bring it up again. I mean, I won't throw it up to you later, when you leave.''

Raider shook his head. "It ain't that easy.''

He pointed toward the church in the middle of the town square. "You're gonna be livin' with the preacher and his family for a while.''

"What!''

"Don't get all excited,'' he replied. "You're a pretty girl, and somebody is gonna come along that you want to marry. Just be patient.''

She picked up her bags. "Goodbye, Raider. I owe you my life. I just wish you loved me more.''

With that, she turned curtly and strode toward the church.

Raider had to admit that it hurt some to see her go. But he was also glad to give up responsibility for her. And as he had said, she wasn't a bad-looking woman. She'd have her pick in a town like Albuquerque.

Raider checked into a clean boardinghouse on the edge of town. He had a good meal and slept through the day and night, all the way to the next morning. When he woke up, he took a long bath and then emptied the widow lady's cupboard, paying extra for the huge breakfast.

Ordinarily Raider stayed at an establishment that could provide him with the three pleasures he enjoyed most in life—whiskey, gambling, and women. but his run-in with Billy Santos and his trail ride with Mindy had left him tired. And he knew the inevitable awaited him in town—the telegram from the home office in Chicago, directing him to a new case.

After his belly was full, he rode into town, taking the time to buy a new set of clothes—a fresh cotton shirt, new denim pants, socks, underwear, and a new Stetson. He could not bring himself to ditch his old boots, so he found a cobbler and waited while new soles and heels were tacked on. The old shoemaker also shined the Justins, remarking about the knife sheath in the right boot. Raider just nodded and flipped him an extra two bits.

Striding down the sidewalk, clean-shaven and smartly attired, Raider attracted the furtive glances of several proper ladies. Of course, the big man from Arkansas did not take much to the kind of women who sipped tea and gossiped over biscuits. He preferred the straight-on type of girl who knew what he wanted and was willing to accept a gratuity to deliver it.

But women would have to wait.

Raider turned into the confines of the Western Union office, nodding at the clerk who remembered him from other messages, other cases.

"Anything come in?" Raider asked, holding his breath.

No telegram meant a few more days—or at least hours—of rest.

The clerk shook his head. "Nope." He smiled. "Don't reckon your boss man knows where you are."

Raider unfolded the report he had written. "Send this in a hurry—you know the routine."

The clerk, a young man, nodded approvingly. "So you put

the qua-eetus on Billy Santos, huh?''

"I did.''

A puzzled look from the clerk. "You don't sound so proud."

"Killin' ain't always somethin' to be proud of.''

The clerk shrugged and started to tap on the operator key.

Raider turned to leave.

"Ain't you gonna wait for the reply?'' the clerk asked.

"I'll be back.''

No need to jump right back into the fire. It was a nice summer day in the mountains. Best to take a walk and enjoy the sun, maybe line up a poker game or maybe a pretty girl for the night.

But Raider only wandered aimlessly through town, his eyes unfocused, his mind a blank.

What the hell was it that was bothering him? He had brought in Santos, or at least a reasonable facsimile. Everybody was happy.

He heard the tolling of the schoolhouse bell.

It was the woman, Mindy. She was still on his mind. He couldn't forget the way she felt next to him. A woman could make a man feel like a king.

Was that why his partner had quit the service to get married?

Raider knew he would never quit.

He found a small stream at the edge of town and watched the children as they caught sunnies on heavy thread and bent pins.

When the sun was high in the blue heavens, the big man got up and started back to the telegraph office.

CHAPTER FOUR

On a bright summer day in Chicago, the Pinkerton Agency was alive with activity. Titus Tilden, assistant to William Wagner and Allan Pinkerton, sat at his desk, gazing thoughtfully onto Fifth Avenue. His desktop was covered with reports and telegrams, the brunt of the paperwork for practically all the agency's field operatives.

Tilden leafed through the reports, reading them all but taking more time with the ones that were particularly interesting. His respect for the men working under him was great, the only exception being one unruly gentleman from Arkansas—Raider. He wondered about the big man, running wild in New Mexico, no doubt riddling the countryside with barrages of lead from his Colt .45.

Tilden adjusted his starched cuffs and then straightened his tie. He tried to encourage all of his operatives to be sharp dressers. Naturally Raider resisted, preferring the traditional style of western garb. It irked Tilden that the big man had his own way of doing things. There were established procedures, points of order for agents to follow. Raider walked the line, barely staying within the guidelines and at times stepping all over them.

When he first hired on as Wagner's assistant, Tilden had wondered how the big man could get away with some of his stunts. He had discussed the irregularities—namely dead bodies that were missing from Raider's brief reports—with Pinkerton and Wagner. They only had one reply: *Raider is good.*

Reluctantly, Tilden had accepted this explanation. Later, he had come to realize that men like Raider were necessary in the wake of lawlessness in the territories. In spite of western expansion, there still existed the type of criminal who stopped at nothing in the way of force to gain his illegal ends. Raider was the fire to fight the fire. And it didn't matter if the flames got out of hand, as long as justice was served and no innocent people were killed.

Tilden leaned back in his chair, exhaling. Justice. Was that what they were really after? Did justice really require the blazing stream of fire from a six-gun? Raider seemed to think it did.

No one knew exactly how many men Raider had killed. Rough estimates ranged from fifty to four hundred, depending on who you wanted to believe. Some said that Doc Weatherbee, Raider's former partner, had a little book with the name of every man Raider had gunned down with his Colt. Before he left the service, Weatherbee had denied this allegation, lending more mystery to Raider's legend.

"Mr. Tilden!"

He looked up to see a messenger coming toward his desk.

"A telegram from New Mexico," the boy said.

Tilden nodded and dismissed the lad. He sat for a while, staring at the dispatch. Raider was in New Mexico. With the big man from Arkansas, the news could be good or bad—or both at the same time.

Tilden unfolded the message. "I, Raider, was sent by the marshal of New Mexico to find Billy Santos who has been robbing and killing all over the territory. He would not come back of his own free will so I killed him and buried his body."

Short and sweet. That was the big man's style. Tilden wondered if the confirmation had arrived from the marshal's office. He decided to send a dispatch to the marshal to be sure.

On his way to lunch, Tilden dropped off the message to the marshal's office. An hour later, he picked up the reply. The authorities in New Mexico confirmed the apprehension of Billy Santos, leaving out the part about the "head in the sack."

Tilden only nodded and went back to his office.

Wagner was waiting for him. Pinkerton wanted to see both of them in his office immediately. Tilden and Wagner took seats opposite the large man's desk, watching as Pinkerton contemplated the task at hand.

Tilden fought the urge to ask his boss to get on with it.

Pinkerton did not make them wait long. "Trouble," he said, giving a raspy chortle. "I suppose trouble is what you might call our main enterprise. We are entrepreneurs of the law."

Wagner adjusted his wire-rimmed spectacles. "Does this have anything to do with that post from Arizona?"

Pinkerton nodded. "Adobe Sands, Arizona. The letter came in this week." He lifted the parchment. "From a Mr. Adrian Thornton."

"What's the nature of the problem?" Tilden asked.

Pinkerton leveled an icy stare at his eager associate. "Killing," he replied. "Murder most foul. Thefts as well, though not as numerous as the killings."

Tilden started to speculate as to the position of the local authorities, but he held his tongue, realizing that any problem dealt to the agency had already been abandoned by the regional constabulary.

Instead, Tilden asked, "Are there any suspects in the killings?"

"Yes," Pinkerton replied. "A priest."

Wagner almost fell out of his chair. "You mean an ordained father of the Catholic Church?"

"I'm assuming he's ordained," Pinkerton replied. "Although there's nothing here to that effect."

Tilden shook his head. "I'm not surprised the locals have kept their hands out of this one."

"According to Thornton, they've tried," Pinkerton explained. "But the priest has a strong base with the local farmers and homesteaders. They keep him hidden."

Wagner leaned back, his face puzzled. "Sounds like a twist on the old Robin Hood theme. This Thornton, is he aboveboard?"

Pinkerton shrugged. "His bank check was good. I did some asking, and he came up clean. He's a land speculator." Pinkerton held up a map for them. "Adobe Sands is here, near the California border. The speculation has something to do with the coming railroad, I'm sure. Apparently Thornton has purchased large tracts of land for that very reason."

Tilden looked dubious.

Pinkerton regarded his subordinate. "Something, Titus?"

"I just thought the railroad was taking a more northerly route. After all, the last spike will be driven soon, connecting the East and the West."

Pinkerton nodded but added, "This type of speculation requires a great deal of time. The landholders are playing a waiting game. They can afford to wait with the cheap price they're paying for the land." He cleared his throat. "But let's not forget that our only concern here is the murders. Titus, who's our closest agent?"

Tilden lowered his head and said something.

"I beg your pardon?" Pinkerton said.

Tilden looked up. "Raider," he said more audibly.

Pinkerton's face registered a half smile. "Send him to Adobe Sands immediately."

Tilden's nostrils flared. "Sir, if I may—"

"You may not," Pinkerton replied. "Wagner?"

The older gentleman nodded. "Raider it is."

They both encouraged Tilden to send a telegram to Albuquerque as soon as possible, directing the big Pinkerton agent to his new case.

CHAPTER FIVE

On his way back into town, Raider stopped by the schoolhouse, watching for Mrs. Amanda Brown, widow. He hid behind a thick tree, his eyes focused on the front steps. Finally, Mindy came out with a broom and swept the stoop. Her hair was done up, and she wore a high-necked dress. It hadn't taken her long to fit in.

When she went inside again, Raider turned away. He couldn't help thinking about her, not after sleeping with her for a week on the trail. He hadn't fully appreciated Mindy when she was beside him. Missing her hurt a lot more than he wanted it to.

Just forget, he told himself, the way you forget about everything else.

He clopped along the wooden sidewalk until he reached the Western Union office. The clerk took his feet down from the desk when Raider walked in. He had been waiting for the big man.

"Ten minutes past closing time," the clerk said. "Almost gave up on you getting back here for your message."

Raider tipped his hat. "Appreciate your waitin'." Raider flipped him a dollar, which was what the kid had really been waiting for.

"Thanks, Mr. Raider."

"Just Raider."

"Thanks." He pocketed the silver. "I figured you'd want this as soon as possible." He handed Raider the communiqué from the home office.

Raider unfolded the paper. "Proceed at once to Adobe Sands,

Arizona, southwest of Kingman near the California border. Contact Mr. Adrian Thornton. Pursue investigation of killings. *Follow all investigative procedures as dictated by this office.* Advise every two weeks as to progress. Titus Tilden."

Raider smiled at the mention of procedure. Tilden was like an old granny lady. An office boy with his butt in a chair. What the hell did he know about slapping leather or facing a man with a moving hand? Had Tilden ever been ambushed by a hidden Winchester?

"Something funny?" the clerk asked.

Raider shook his head. "Not really."

He glanced up at the kid. For a minute he considered asking him about the possibilities in Albuquerque after the sun went down. He decided somebody as young as the clerk wouldn't be versed yet in the finer arts of gambling and whoring. *Proceed at once.* He didn't have much time.

"Adios," he said to the kid.

"When will you be back this way, Raider?"

"Don't strain your neck lookin' for me," Raider called back over his shoulder.

On the way back to the boardinghouse, Raider stopped at the livery where he had stabled the black stallion. He had left specific orders with the blacksmith to put out the word that the black had been stolen by Billy Santos and anyone who could identify the brand could claim the horse. According to the smithy, the brand wasn't a regular marking of the region, and no one had shown up to claim the horse anyway.

Raider thanked the smithy and paid up the bill, telling the smithy he'd be there first thing in the morning to ride out.

When he got back to the boardinghouse, the widow woman had dinner ready. Raider stuffed himself with country-fried steak, potatoes, green peas, and thick-cut tomatoes. The widow seemed to take pride in his appetite, serving him second helpings until he pushed away from the table. Raider's dinner partners, other residents of the boardinghouse, also watched with curiosity as the tall man rose from the table and tromped up the stairs.

Raider wanted to sleep some before he went out on the town. He leaned back on the feather mattress, something he would probably not be able to do for a while after he left Albuquerque.

The soft mattress felt good against his tired back. Was he getting old? How long before the trail took its final toll? He closed his eyes, deciding not to think about it.

His slumber was dreamless. He opened his eyes to darkness. How long had he slept? He listened for sounds of movement in the boardinghouse. Everyone was asleep. He could hear the widow snoring down the hall.

"Damn!"

He sat up on the edge of the bed, wondering if he had missed all the excitement in town. It would have been hard enough to find entertainment on a weeknight, and most of that would be closed down by midnight. When he looked out his window, the full moon hung low in the sky. Too late for adventure in Albuquerque. Leaning back on the bed, he decided to go back to sleep.

He drifted slowly toward a comfortable darkness until he heard the shuffling of feet outside his door.

Raider sat up. Maybe it was just the widow lady going to the toilet. The footsteps stopped next to his door. Raider reached back for his Colt on the bedpost.

Maybe it wasn't going to be a dull evening after all.

The doorknob turned.

Raider slipped against the wall, his hand full of the Peacemaker.

Light from the hallway spilled into his room as the door opened.

Had someone come to avenge Billy Santos's demise?

A head pushed into the room.

Raider grabbed a thin neck and spun the small figure around, pinning it to the wall, lifting the Colt in the intruder's face.

A woman cried out, her wide brown eyes staring at the bore of the .45.

"Mindy!"

He let go of her and closed the door.

Mindy gasped for breath. "What's wrong with you?"

"Shh." Raider eased the Colt back into the holster. "I don't take kindly to people sneaking up on me in the dark."

A knock at the door. Both of them froze as the widow woman asked what was going on inside Raider's room. He replied that he had been having a nightmare. That seemed to satisfy the widow lady, who moved back to her own room.

Raider put his lips close to Mindy's ear. "See what you done. If she catches me with a woman in here, I'll never be able to stay in this place again."

Mindy wrapped her arms around his waist. "Oh, don't be such a fusser. I just came to say goodbye. I couldn't leave things the way they stood."

He had to admit that she felt warm and soft against his body. But he had to push her away from him. "You're a schoolmarm now, Mindy. You can't be sneakin' in here, beddin' down with me. You got to act proper now."

Her lower lip protruded. "Proper. I had me a belly full of proper already. That preacher and his wife are so pious it kills me."

Raider wasn't sure what "pious" meant, but it didn't sound like anything he wanted to be a part of. "It's only been one day, Mindy."

Mindy slid her hands behind his head. "I just wanted one more time before I have to start walking the straight and narrow."

Raider wanted one more time as well.

He grabbed the blanket from the bed. "Can't do it here."

"Why not?"

"We'll make too much noise," he replied.

She pressed her mouth against his. Raider kissed her for a few seconds and then broke away. He had to get her out of the boardinghouse before the widow found them together.

"Where then?" Mindy asked.

"I know a place by a creek," he replied. "It's a warm night. No one will catch us there."

She giggled, as if she loved the idea.

As they snuck out of the house, Raider felt guilty and excited at the same time. Another tumble with Mindy was what he wanted in the first place. He wondered how she would feel after she went back under the preacher's watchful eye. A schoolmarm had everyone in the town pretty much looking up her ass twenty-four hours a day.

The air was warm outside. They hurried through the darkness, making for the creek where Raider had been earlier in the day. The long walk only served to hone the edge of their need.

Raider found a thick spot of grass and spread out the blanket. He could hear the rustling brook as the water rushed over the rocky bed. The moon was still high enough to illumine Mrs. Amanda Brown's lovely face.

Raider touched her cheek. "You're a beautiful woman."

She shrugged. "Then stay here and marry me."

He laughed. "You're a sight more plucky than the day I found you sittin' by your sister's grave."

Mindy frowned, looking away from him.

"Sorry," he said softly.

Her brown eyes lifted to meet his penitent expression. "I'm glad all of that is over. I didn't want my sister to die, but I always did think it was crazy to come out here. I guess I came because there was no place else to go."

"It ain't worked out all that bad," he offered. "You looked pretty sweeping the steps of the school today."

She raised an eyebrow. "Spying on me."

"I was just passin' by."

She kissed the corner of his mouth. "You're sweet. If you ever decide to come back this way . . . ooh . . ."

Raider embraced her, grabbing her backside, pulling her in close to him, nipping at the tender places of her neck.

Suddenly she didn't feel like talking anymore.

They took it slow at first, undressing, freeing their bodies to bathe in the warm night. He touched her breasts before he pulled her against him. He felt the hair between her thighs bumping the head of his prick.

"Let's lay down," he entreated.

Mindy laughed. "You're going to have to work harder than that." She gave him a playful push and ran toward the stream.

"Hey!"

The big man felt like a fool, just standing there in the moonlight with his dick hanging out.

Mindy giggled all the way to the creek, where she waded into the cold water. Raider stepped gingerly over the rocks, edging next to the stream. The foolish woman dived headlong into the stream, stroking a few feet with the current.

"Are you loco?" he called.

She stood up and splashed cold water on him. "If you want me, you have to come get me."

There was enough moonlight for Raider's black eyes to perceive the white outline of her breasts.

"Come on out of there, Mindy."

She splashed him again. Raider lost his temper, wading in after her. Mindy dived back into the current, swimming for the deep pool fifty feet downstream. Raider had no choice but to swim after her.

His body felt frozen at first. But as he moved along in the creek, he gradually became used to the frigid water. He heard Mindy giggling to his right. Her head bobbed up and down.

Raider slid next to her, grabbing her shoulder, pulling her against him. He felt the softness of her body as his prick bumped against the crack of her buttocks. Mindy reached back for his cock, undoing some of the damage done by the cold water. As Raider grew harder, she thrust her bottom backward.

"You sure you want to try it?" he whispered. "It might hurt."

"Just a little," she moaned.

But a little was too much. Raider had also grown tired of their aquatic antics. He swam her to shore and picked her up in his arms, carrying her across the grass to the blanket.

Raider eased her down on the blanket. Her chill-bumped thighs spread out. Raider lowered his wet body, settling into the notch of her cunt. Mindy grabbed his cock and guided it to the entrance of her pink crevice.

"It's a little dry," she whispered. "Take it slow, and remember to pull out at the right time."

He sunk his length into her, slowly filling her up. Mindy groaned and started to squirm beneath him. Her head lolled from side to side, her teeth bared and white in the diminishing moonlight.

Raider waited as long as he could before he withdrew his cock and spilled his discharge on her stomach. That wasn't the end of it, though. Mindy wiped the head of his prick and stroked it until he was hard again.

"Roll over on your back," she insisted.

"What are you doin', woman?"

"Just do it. I want to try somethin' I used to do with my husband."

Raider obeyed her, dutifully reclining on the damp blanket.

Mindy straddled his crotch, gripping his massive member. She guided the head to her cunt, slipping the tip inside her labia. "Now," she moaned. She sat down on his cock, shivering as she hit bottom.

Raider helped her along. He grabbed her ass and lifted her up and down. She caught on quickly, bouncing off him with a surprising deftness. She worked on him for a long time, but she could not get him to come again.

"Don't you like it?" she asked.

"Yeah. But . . . I don't know, I like to be on top."

She lifted herself off him and stretched out beside his lean body. "Then do it. Get on top of me and do it like you did to the dirtiest whore you've ever known."

His brow wrinkled a little. "Mindy, where did you learn to talk like that? I mean . . ."

"Oh, just hush. I'm not that much different than you. Are you going to do it or not?"

He rolled over, settling again between her thighs. "Going to do it."

His prick jabbed at her until he found the mark. She drew air through her tight lips as he penetrated her. A shiver ran through every inch of her body.

"Don't forget to pull out."

That set him off. Raider pulled up her legs, balancing her calves on his shoulders. His hips rose and fell, driving her ass against the soft tuft of grass covered by the blanket. Mindy cried out so loudly that he wondered if her echoes might reach all the way back to town. All he needed was to get caught topping the new schoolmarm. He'd never be welcomed in Albuquerque again.

The tightness of her cunt made him forget such thoughts. He continued his steady rhythm, rising toward his own climax. As he felt his second discharge nearing, he waited a few seconds more before starting to withdraw.

Mindy shuddered as his cock came out. When he had

finished, she drew him back in, quivering as he re-entered. They just lay there by the brook, catching their breaths from the pleasurable effort.

Raider reclined next to her, putting an arm around her. Mindy rolled over, throwing a leg up on his thigh. Her face pressed into his chest.

"I'm gonna miss you, Raider."

He had a speech worked out. He was going to say a lot of nice things and then tell her about how his job was the most important thing in his life. How he could never be true to just one woman because it went against his nature. He'd also malign his own qualifications as a husband, telling her that he didn't make a whole lot of money and that he couldn't do much else beyond chasing badmen. He knew very little about farming or building or raising livestock. Hell, horses usually died under him, either from being ridden too hard or from bullet wounds.

The whole speech was planned to spare her feelings. At the end he would tell her that if he ever was going to settle down, it would be with somebody like Mindy. A kind speech. The only trouble was, he never got a chance to deliver it.

A rifle exploded in the night. Slugs thudded into the blanket next to the big man, digging into the springy turf. Raider pushed Mindy off the blanket and then rolled away himself. He didn't have his Colt with him. He reached for his boot, grabbing the hunting knife he kept in a special sheath on the right side.

The rifle continued enough for Raider to mark the direction of the muzzle flashes.

He raised the knife. Not much weaponry against a Winchester. Still, it was all he had.

"Stay put," he whispered to the trembling woman.

He got up and ran naked into the moon shadows of the warm night.

The rifle shots had come from a small clump of rocks upstream. Raider ran toward the rocks. circling wide to avoid the bushwhacker. Who the hell was trying to kill him?

As he drew closer to the hiding place of the sniper, Raider stopped and bent low. The moon, which had been riding the edge of the horizon, had sunk halfway into the earth. If he could wait just a little longer, he might have a better chance in the dark.

The last sliver of the moon disappeared, deepening the shadowed patches of black. It did not matter, though. Raider heard him coming., He tiptoed out of the rocks, moving along the bank of the stream.

Raider put the hunting knife in his teeth. The water was his only chance. And the rifleman had to stay close to the bank. Better to just go, try it without thinking. Sometimes, when your ass was to the wall, you just had to move quick.

As the rifleman kept going, Raider moved up behind him, slipping into the water. He floated with the current, listening for the crunching of boot soles on creek pebbles. Mindy would be in a heap of trouble if the sniper reached her first.

The Comanches had a neat trick that Raider had learned the hard way. A Comanche brave would wait in the water until you came up to take a drink. He'd breathe through a reed, hunkering under the surface like a submerged alligator. As you cupped your hand into the water, the brave would leap up and drag you into the drink.

When Raider heard the man's boots, he slid out of the creek and grabbed an ankle. His lungs whooped a Rebel war cry, half in fear, half to scare the unknown asssailant. Raider pulled hard on the ankle, tripping the rifleman and sending him to the ground.

The rifle exploded as the man fell. Raider jabbed the tip of the knife in the man's knee. A loud cry from the stuck bushwhacker. He pulled away, leaving Raider with an empty boot.

A clicking rifle lever sent Raider back into the deep pool. Slugs rained down on the water. Raider could see the muzzle flashes even with his head buried in the pool. The ambusher was standing confidently over the creek, firing blindly.

Raider counted the shots until he was sure the Winchester had fired its limit. He raised up out of the water, screaming like a wildcat. The rifleman fumbled with a cartridge, trying to load it before Raider reached him.

The big man didn't take any chances. He hurled the hunting knife in the direction of the muzzle flashes. Did he hear a grunt and a wet breath?

When the rifle went off, Raider dived again, expecting the pool to bubble with flying lead. But there were no more shots. Raider lifted his head out of the water. Random steps on the rocky bank. A human form splashed into the creek.

Anticipating a trick, Raider moved slowly toward the corpse. He finally had to catch the dead man to keep him from floating downstream. The hunting knife had hit him just under the throat.

He dragged the body to shore and went to look for Mindy. He found her stretched out on the blanket, trembling. Kneeling beside her, he put his hand on her cheek and assured her that everything was all right.

"Do it to me," she cried, "Hurry."

Raider found that he was ready. He mounted her and finished quickly. This time he did not withdraw at the moment of climax. Mindy did not seem to care. She squirmed under him, releasing the rest of her demons.

"We can't wait too long," Raider said. "You got to get up and get dressed. Head on back to the preacher's house."

He stood up, looking for their clothes.

"I'll go for the marshal," Mindy said.

"No! Just get on home."

"But why?"

Raider stepped into his pants., "What are you going to tell him? That we were taking a walk out here? Don't worry, I'll handle everything. You just go back where you belong."

They hurried, somehow managing to find their clothes in the darkness.

When she was fully dressed, Mindy threw her arms around Raider's waist. "I reckon this is goodbye."

"Don't make more of it than there is," Raider replied. "Just get on back to town. As you might be able to tell, I'm not exactly the safest person to be around."

She let go of him. "I can't argue with that. Goodbye, Raider. I won't ever forget you."

Without further ado, she hurried back toward town. Raider pulled on his boots and ran back to the creek to look for the body. He had to walk downstream until he tripped over the corpse.

He picked up the rifle, which was out of ammunition. Not that he needed bullets, with the hole in the man's gullet. With a tentative hand, he pulled out the hunting knife and dipped it in the creek. He dried the blade on the dead man's poncho.

Raider searched the ground for the man's hat. A sombrero. Mexican. Billy Santos had been half Mexican. Maybe the marshal would know the dead man. Maybe he could piece it together.

The big man started back toward town, walking the same path that Mindy had taken. As he clipped along, he wondered how the rifleman had found him in the darkness. Damn it all, the gunplay had taken most of the fun out of his last fling with Mindy. Most, but not all.

Raider blew out an exhausted jet of air. What the hell could happen next? He knew the answer to that question when he saw the riders coming toward him. Torches burned high in the air. Four of them. A posse?

The marshal rode up to him, glaring down from the saddle of a chestnut filly. "Raider! I mighta knowed you'd be around. Somebody heard shootin' out this way. Woke us all from a dead sleep."

Raider nodded. "Well, you didn't get up for nothin'. I was, er, takin' me a little walk. Couldn't sleep. Somebody followed me, tried to bushwhack me."

"Where is he?" the lawman asked.

Raider pointed back toward the creek. "Lyin' yonder. Mexican. Had to take him with my knife."

"Let's go look."

The marshal's tone carried a note of inevitable defeat. Raider swung up into the saddle behind one of the other riders. They pounded the trail to the creek, gliding along the bank until the torches illuminated the body of the ambusher.

Raider and the marshal climbed down to examine the corpse. The marshal went through the man's pockets, finding a few coins and superstitious charms. He held up a pendant that looked like a mountain lion's claw on a leather thong.

"Apache all right," the lawman said.

Raider nodded. "I figured there was somebody out there who liked Billy."

The marshal waved the torch over the man's face. "Can't say that I know him."

"Was Billy knowed to ride with anybody else?" Raider asked.

"Some say he did," declared one of the riders. It was the weak-faced deputy. "Some say he had a cousin on his Mexican side."

"Don't matter none," the marshal replied. "You boys get this one on back to town. Take him over to the undertaker."

"We ain't got an extra horse," replied the weak-faced man.

"Double up!" the marshal snapped. "Unless one of you wants a dead man ridin' behind you."

The weak-faced man doubled up with a deputy on a gray, giving the dead man his own mount.

The funeral procession started back toward town, lighted by the three torches over the riders' heads.

When they were gone, the marshal spun back toward Raider, pointing a finger. "Now don't take this the wrong way, Raider. I like you just fine. Ever' time you do a job for me, you finish it. But you also get into more trouble than a raccoon with two peckers."

Raider sort of hung his head, pretending remorse. "I know, Marshal. And I sure am sorry. Maybe I ought to just get back to bed."

"Maybe you ought to just get out of town!"

Raider nodded. It was time to leave anyway. He asked the marshal for a ride, but the lawman offered Raider his own horse. He would walk back. And Raider had better be gone by the time he got there!

CHAPTER SIX

Raider decided to ride all the way to Arizona. The trains hadn't gone that far yet, although it seemed like they were spreading out tracks in every corner of the southwest territory. Raider hated trains. They stunk worse than any horse he had ever ridden, and the cinders always found their way into the corner of his eye, stinging and burning until he cried like a baby to get them out. The motion of the train always played hell with the big man's stomach, too, leaving him nauseous and weak-legged after a long ride on a rocking boxcar.

Stagecoaches weren't much better. They were slower than the train, more cramped, and always breaking a wheel or an axle. Summer rains could stir up enough soupy mud to mire down a Concord coach, prompting the driver to ask any male passengers, especially big men, to stand knee deep in the muck and push hard. Raider liked to avoid stagecoaches whenever possible.

So he saddled up the black stallion and left Albuquerque before the sun had risen behind him. The good weather held to the Arizona border, where Raider left New Mexico grasslands for the arid plain of the sun-baked territory. The black took the heat better than Raider had figured he would. As long as the big man kept him at a slow, steady pace, the strong-backed animal held his head high, plodding over the dusty plain.

The routine was always the same. Rise before the sun, push forward until the hot part of the day. Rest the animal (and himself) until the afternoon breezes picked up. Ride until dark,

make a fire if there was any wood available, or just go straight
to sleep if there wasn't.

He lived on jerky, wild plants, and any small game he could
kill with his rifle. Raider tried to refrain from killing deer and
antelope because they were usually too large to be eaten at one
sitting. He didn't have time to strip out the meat and dry it for
jerky.

Proceed at once. Sometimes Raider wondered if he was like
a piece on a chessboard. Tilden moved him around from place
to place, the pawn with a six-gun. Raider wasn't sure how to
play chess, but he figured the principle was the same.

He stayed with the mountains for a while, finding plenty of
water in the local streams. The rain had been heavier than
usual, so there was a lot of runoff from the lofty peaks. He
would sit by some rivers during the hot part of the day, watching
as lazy cutthroat trout rose to the surface, popping at a bug or
a grub that floated in the current. Raider had never cared much
for fish, so he passed up any attempt to catch the colorful
creatures, choosing instead to hunt jackrabbits with his Winchester. The meat was good after it had hung over a fire for a
couple of hours.

At the end of his second week on the trail, Raider happened
on a prospector who pointed the way to Kingman. He asked
the grizzled old gold-hound about the approximate location of
Adobe Sands, but the prospector had never heard of it. Raider
just tipped his Stetson and kept plugging, making his slow way
across the sweltering plain.

The heat could do strange things to a man. He'd see something and ride like hell to get there. But he'd never reach his
destination. The mirage would disappear in the wavy lines of
heat that rose off the ground.

Raider didn't pay much attention to the dark structures that
seemed to grow out of the bare flatland ahead of him. He just
kept his eyes low, shading his face from the sun with the brim
of his Stetson. He knew the town wasn't a mirage when he
saw a hand-painted sign that declared, KINGMAN, TERRITORY
OF ARIZONA. The sign was weathered and decayed, as if no
one had been out to tend it for a while.

In Kingman, the sheriff pointed him southwest, urging Raider to head on immediately. It didn't matter that the big man said he was an agent for Allan Pinkerton. The sheriff simply didn't want a gun-toting man to hang around and cause trouble. Raider insisted he wouldn't make any noise, but the sheriff insisted that there were a few hotheads around who might want to draw down on a Pinkerton just to try it.

Raider watered his horse, bought some more jerky, and obeyed the sheriff's wishes. Still, the big man could not help but feel that Pinkerton agents sometime got the short end of the stick. Pinks were blamed for a lot of things that they did not do or that they were forced to do by the men they were chasing. He simply put Kingman behind him, taking a south-westerly direction toward Adobe Sands.

The sign had been freshly painted with big, square letters announcing, ADOBE SANDS, ARIZONA. TOWN OF OPPORTU-NITY.

Raider shook his head as he passed the sign. Adobe Sands looked like the last place on earth where opportunity would choose to put down roots. The black, as steady as he was at the beginning of the journey, clopped onto the dusty street that served as the main thoroughfare for the gray little town. Raider counted less than ten structures, but noted happily that one of the buildings was a saloon.

Across the street from the saloon was a livery where a dozen or so people had gathered for some kind of dispute. Raider heard their voices resounding in the hot air, fueling the noontime fire. A tall, lanky man with a long scar on his cheek seemed to be arguing with a balding man who had the look of a sodbuster.

Raider just kept coming. When someone saw him and pointed out his presence to the rest of the group, they all turned for a moment to watch him ride in. He payed them little mind, figuring their argument had nothing to do with him. He did, however, mark the presence of a .45-caliber Buntline special on the hip of the scarred man.

After the big man had swung out of the saddle, the argument resumed behind him. He could still hear the voices as he pushed through the double doors of the saloon. A broad-shouldered bartender with greasy hair glanced up at him as he came toward the bar.

"Closed," the bartender said. "Open at two."

Raider was in no mood to argue. He lifted a silver dollar so the man could see it shine. "Eight bits if you pour me a whiskey. I'm dry and hot."

The bartender licked his lips. "Whiskey ain't but two bits."

Raider smiled like a coyote. "Then that leaves six bits for you, don't it."

A shot glass hit the bar. The bartender filled it and pushed it toward Raider. The big man put the silver dollar on the bar. He emptied the glass and plopped down another dollar.

"Got anythin' besides whiskey?" he asked.

The bartender shrugged. "Warm beer."

Raider shook his head and then asked, "How much for this bottle?"

The bartender pushed the red-eye toward him. "Keep waterin' till you had your fill."

Raider poured himself a second shot.

"Don't get many big spenders in here," the bartender offered.

Raider grimaced. "Mister, if you had been ridin' in this heat as long as I have, you'd give your last piece of silver for a drink. Got any water to chase this?"

The bartender reached for a jug behind the counter. He poured a big glass of cool water for Raider, who emptied it as quickly as he had the shot glasss. He motioned for another helping of water.

"Awful dry, ain't you?" the bartender said.

Raider nodded, smiling. "Spittin' cotton."

He drank again and then looked at the slick-haired man behind the bar. Maybe he'd be the one to ask about . . . who the hell was he supposed to see? He started to reach for the slip of paper in his pocket, but a woman's screaming stopped him.

Raider spun back toward the door. "What's goin' on over there?" he asked.

The bartender slunk down low. "Nothin' you or me want to get in the middle of, stranger. Take my word for it."

But the woman screamed again. Raider thought he heard scuffling. Then knuckles cracked on bone, like someone had thrown a fist.

Raider started toward the double doors.

"I mean it, mister," the bartender called. "Just stay out of it if you know what's good for you."

Raider adjusted his Colt. He never liked to hear a woman screaming. Maybe it wasn't his fight, but he could at least have a look. Besides, the disturbance was happening in front of the livery, and the big man had to stable his horse anyway.

"Don't say I didn't warn you!" the bartender cried.

Raider pushed through the double doors and stepped out into the dusty street.

The spectators parted as Raider led the black toward the stable. The man with the scar on his cheek glanced up, looking away from the smaller man who had fallen victim to a well-thrown fist. Raider stopped, keeping his eyes on the Buntline in the scarred man's holster.

"You got a problem?" the scarred man asked.

Raider tipped back his Stetson. "Just want to stable my horse."

The smaller man on the ground scurried to his feet. His woman, a Mexican girl, put her arms around him. She used a handkerchief to wipe the blood from her man's mouth.

Raider nodded toward the hurt man. "What seems to be the trouble here?"

Scar put a finger in Raider's face. "Ain't no truck of your'n."

"You lookin' to lose that finger?" Raider challenged.

The scar man squared his shoulders, prompting the spectators to move back. His hand hung low by the Buntline. Gray eyes challenged Raider. Eyes that rarely were challenged back.

Raider's hand relaxed over the butt of his Peacemaker. "You can try me if you want, boy. But you just might lose more'n that finger."

The scar relaxed into a smile. "You're somethin' of a bad-ass, ain't you, big man."

"Bad for them that wants it," Raider replied. He nodded again toward the bleeding sodbuster. "S'pose you tell me what this man done to make you beat up on him.''

The scar pointed a finger at the balding man. "Why don't you ask him? He knows what he done.''

Raider eyed the small man. "Tell me quick, pardner.''

"I ain't done a thing!" the man cried. "I come to get my horse from the livery so I can clear out of this godforsaken town. Me and Carmelita are headin' back to Texas. Then Clanton here"—he indicated the man with the scar—"he says I got to leave my horse. Says I can't take him.''

"You pay the livery?" Raider asked.

The man nodded. "Two bucks, includin' shoes.''

Raider sighed. "All right, boy. Take your horse and clear on out of here.''

The man called Clanton reached for the tether of a big harness-bred, which was the horse in question. "He ain't leavin' till he tells me where to find that killing padre.''

Raider's brow wrinkled. "Padre?''

"I don't know nothin' about it!" the bleeding man replied.

Clanton raised the crooked finger in the smaller man's face. "He's lyin'. Him and the rest of them homesteaders have been hidin' that murderin' preacher for weeks. He ain't gettin' this horse until he tells me where I can find him.''

"I'm tellin' you," the small man said, "I don't know nothin'.''

Clanton started to slap him. Raider grabbed the scarred man's wrist. There was a struggle. Clanton went for his gun. Raider twisted him around and somehow ended up with the Buntline in hand. Two men behind Clanton went for their guns. Raider stopped them with the bore of the Buntline.

"Anybody feel like dyin' today?" he asked.

Clanton squirmed away from him. "This ain't no business of yours, big man. You're gonna be sorry you got into this.''

Raider shrugged. "That might be so. But you might be surprised at how much of this concerns me." He gestured with the elongated barrel of the Buntline. "Go on, boy," he said to the sodbuster. "Take your horse and git on back to Texas. Go on.''

Hesitantly, the smaller man took the tether of the harness-bred. "Much obliged, mister." He glared at Clanton. "I'm happy to be the hell out of a town that's run by the likes of this polecat!''

Clanton made a menacing move toward the sodbuster, but Raider held him off with the pistol. As the sodbuster moved away with his wife and horse, the other spectators gave a little round of applause for the big Pinkerton. Raider shook his head, wondering what had possessed him to get into a skirmish his first hour in town. What if Clanton had been right and the small man had been shielding a killer? Raider still didn't like the idea of a small man getting pushed around by superior odds. The others didn't seem to want any part of Clanton as well.

The gray eyes glared straight through Raider. ''You're mighty big with that gun in your hand,'' Clanton muttered. ''Maybe you'd like to put down the iron and face me head on. Fist to fist.''

Raider grinned. ''Now, that might not be a bad way to settle all this, Clanton. You any kin to Ike Clanton?''

''Cousin of mine. Never met him, though.''

Raider gestured toward the two gunhands who were standing behind the scarred man. ''Say you and me face off. What about these two boys here? They just gonna sit by and knit while we're mixin' it up.''

Both of Clanton's sidekicks looked like they wanted to draw on Raider.

Clanton motioned for them to leave. ''Go tell the boss we got us a peck of trouble here.''

They hesitated, but then nodded and moved off.

Clanton grinned, showing his brown teeth. ''Now, big 'un, you ain't got no excuse to chicken out on me.''

Raider handed the Buntline to one of the spectators. He took off his gunbelt and hung it over the saddle horn of the black. He hung his Stetson on the butt of his Winchester, which was still in the scabbard.

''Let's go, Clanton,'' he said finally, raising his fists.

The spectators circled up, forming a ring around the two contestants.

Some of the fire was gone from Clanton's eyes. But he raised his fists, swinging them in the air. Raider stepped forward and drew a mark on the ground with his foot.

"Toe up, Clanton."

"What?"

Raider grinned. "Rules, you know. First one can't put his foot on the mark is the loser. Or ain't you ever fought fair before?"

Clanton replied by rushing the big man. His wild, roundhouse blows were easy to avoid. Raider used skills that had been honed by years of fighting, keeping his balance, stepping from side to side with fancy footwork.

"Stand still, damn you!" Clanton cried.

Raider obliged him, only Clanton probably wished he hadn't. Raider flipped a left hand into Clanton's nose, knocking him to the ground with the first punch. The scarred man got up with blood pouring from his nostrils. Raider thought he might give it up, but there wasn't any quit in him.

Clanton charged again, tackling Raider's legs. They wrestled on the ground, neither of them able to gain an advantage. Finally Raider got enough leverage in his legs to kick Clanton off him. He stood up, waiting for the lanky roughhouser to stand up. Clanton staggered to his feet.

"Had enough, Clanton?"

"I'm gonna kill you, big man. I'm gonna kill you with my bare hands."

Raider hammered a right hand to the hard part of Clanton's skull. A mistake, the big man thought as he heard his knuckles crunching. His hand stung like it had been put through a cotton gin.

In the moment of hesitation that accompanied the pain, Clanton gained a slight advantage. He swung a fist into Raider's gut, forcing the big man onto one knee. Clanton lifted his foot, popping it into Raider's chest, knocking him down on the ground.

Raider groaned, rolling to his right as Clanton's boot came after him. He felt like he was going to throw up his guts. Clanton put the hard toe in the small of Raider's back, numbing the nerves in his lower body.

"How's that feel, you big tub of horse shit!" Clanton cried. "Get up and fight like a man!"

He made the mistake of letting Raider regain his feet. Clanton tried to stay on top of him, throwing a barrage of punches that Raider caught on his upraised arms. He had to keep Clanton off long enough to get back some of his strength.

Clanton had other ideas. He swung hard, battering the big man's face, stinging him like an angry wasp. Raider had to do something quick or he'd end up in the water trough behind him.

Clanton came around with a haymaker that didn't connect. The scarred man lost his balance, stumbling a few steps. Raider grabbed him, gripping his body in a bear hug. Clanton grunted, trying to break free, but Raider was too strong for him.

As Raider squeezed the breath from his lungs, Clanton's face turned red and then blue. Some of the spectators would swear later that they heard bones breaking. When Raider released him, Clanton fell to the ground, panting like a dog.

Raider stepped over and toed the mark. "Now, let's fight, boy. Come on, if you still got it in you."

He still had it in him.

They circled around, stalking each other. Clanton tried the rushing move again, but this time he met Raider's straight left. The blow caught the scar squarely, staggering Raider's lanky adversary. Clanton still tried to fight back, swinging his arms in an ineffective windmill motion. Raider avoided the awkward punches, slamming rights and lefts into Clanton's face and body.

Blood gushed from Clanton's mouth, but he still refused to give up. He toed the mark, lifting his fists. Raider felt bad about hitting him, but he had no choice as Clanton's wild blows rained down on him.

Raider backed him up toward the water trough, battering the man until he was no longer strong enough to lift his arms. Clanton fell like a chopped-down tree, splashing into the water. He floated in the drink, squirming but unable to get out of the trough. Raider went over and dropped his foot on the mark, prompting cheers from the dozen spectators.

Raider looked back toward Clanton, who was in no shape to keep fighting. He had to hand it to the lanky man— he didn't know how to quit. His arms were still flailing blindly at the breeze.

"When he comes around, give him back his Buntline,"

Raider called to the man who was holding the gun.

He started toward the stallion. Another onlooker stepped in to take the animal to the livery. Raider had to move lively to get his gunbelt and his Stetson from the saddle. He had made some friends in Adobe Sands. They moved in to pat him on the back and shake his hand.

Raider endured the congratulations just to be polite. When they were tapering off, he started for the saloon, followed by several of the spectators. They wanted to buy him drinks, to find out who he was and why he had come to Adobe Sands.

The bartender gaped at the crowd as they rushed through the swinging doors. He poured warm beer and red-eye for them, dropping the coins into his kitty. He also shook Raider's hand, taking back the warning he had given earlier. He had to brag on the winner.

"Watched the whole thing through the window," he said to the others. "Never thought I'd see the day when somebody gave that bully Clanton a taste of his own medicine!"

Raider gulped down the whiskey as if it were a tincture for pain. "He gave me a good run," the big man replied. "It was close any way you look at it."

"Yeah," one of the barflies rejoined, "but you come out on top. Winner and champeen!"

Raider felt his jaw, moving it back and forth. He didn't like fighting as much as he had in his younger days. He told himself to remember not to hit anyone in the hard part of the head again.

But the pain seemed to ease as the drinks went down. Being surrounded by a hoard of well-wishers helped him some. It was easier to come out of a fight as the victor, no matter how much you hurt afterward.

The big man from Arkanssas lifted his glass. "Hit me again, barkeep."

As the bartender poured him another ration of red-eye, Raider looked around at the men who drank with him. They were simple types, like the sodbuster who had cleared out with his horse and his woman. Raider recalled something about a padre, a murdering preacher. Clanton had said it. Did the others know anything about it? Did it have anything to do with the reason

Raider had been sent to Adobe Sands? Whatever reason that was.

He had to start asking questions. The fight had been a good thing if it could win the confidence of the townfolk. He eyed the bartender, thinking he would be a good place to begin.

But before he could direct his inquiry at him, the bartender straightened up and glared toward the swinging doors.

"Judas Priest!" the barkeeper cried.

The others made similar exclamations and backed away from Raider.

Spinning around, Raider glared at the staggering figure of the man he had bested in the fight. Clanton teetered in the door, his hand full of the Buntline. The bore of the long-barreled weapon was pointing toward the floor. Raider drew his Colt and thumbed back the hammer.

"You come far enough," the big man said. "Don't make me kill you."

Clanton staggered into the barroom, still holding the weapon. He spit blood into the sawdust on the floor. Everyone held their breath, wondering what he was going to do. Clanton just smiled and dropped the Buntline into his holster. Was the fight really gone out of him?

"I come to have a drink with the man who whupped me," Clanton said.

Raider did not holster his Colt right away. "You sure that's all you come for, Clanton?"

"Call me Ace," the brown-toothed man replied. "Ever'body else does."

The townies moved away as Clanton strode up to the bar.

"Whiskey," he said, " and make it quick. This boy done put a hurtin' on me that I ain't likely to forget."

The bartender filled a shot glass and slid it toward the bruised Clanton. He drank it in one gulp and asked for another. The second shot went down just as quickly.

"Four bits," the bartender demanded.

"It's on me," Raider replied.

Clanton offered his hand. Raider took it. He could never fault a man who wanted to make good after a whipping. It worked out that way sometimes. One minute a man was trying to kill you, the next minute he was drinking with you like he was your best friend. A certain kind of man respected anyone who could take him in a fistfight.

Clanton focused his gray eyes on the big Pinkerton. "I'm figurin' you ain't here in Adobe Sands to find a square dance, big 'un."

Raider nodded. He noticed that the others had moved away. They weren't sure if they should trust him now that he was drinking with Ace Clanton. Still, he figured Clanton might be a good place to start with his questions.

"Nope," Raider replied, "I'm here on business. Come on behalf of a man named . . . now what the hell was his name?"

Raider reached into his vest pocket and withdrew a small piece of paper. "Got to see a Mr. Adrian Thornton," he said. "Know him?"

Clanton squinted at the man who had knocked him senseless. "You must be the Pinkerton he sent for."

Raider nodded. "One and the same. How'd you know?"

A brown-mouthed smile from Clanton. "Thornton's the man who just about owns this town, pardner." He slugged down the last gulp of red-eye. "Come on, I'll take you to him right now. He's been waitin' for somebody to come in and clear this up. I been tryin' myself, but it ain't worked out so good."

Clanton started off until Raider stopped him. "How do you know this Thornton, Ace?"

Again the brown smile. "Let's just say that, as of now, we're both workin' for the same man, big 'un."

Clanton's laugh made Raider uneasy. What the hell had Tilden gotten him into this time? Despite the churning in his gut, Raider felt the best thing to do was follow Clanton.

He fell in behind the lanky man, following him out of the bar, leaving the townfolk to whisper their doubts among themselves.

CHAPTER SEVEN

As they strode down the dusty street, Raider got a better view of the "Town of Opportunity." It looked like a shadow of the kind of "boom town" that had grown up during the gold rush and the homesteading run. Not much of it was left. The saloon and livery were still open, but the other stores and businesses had long since vanished. A seedy general store sat next to an old hotel, a sign in the window declaiming: OPEN SATURDAY ONLY, A.T. Adrian Thornton? Raider wondered.

He stopped and pointed to the sign. "Thornton own the general store too?" he asked clanton.

"What do you think?" came the offhand reply.

Why the hell would anybody want to own anything in Adobe Sands?

Clanton gestured toward the door of the hotel. "Come on in, big man. Get out of the sun."

"Call me Raider."

Clanton laughed. "Good name for a man like you."

"Sure enough, Ace."

They went into the hotel. The lobby had been abandoned. No one at the desk. No customers, as far as Raider could tell. Clanton told him to wait by the desk for a minute.

When he was alone, Raider stole a peek at the closed sign-in book. The last name had been registered over a year ago. Thornton sure as hell didn't seem to be operating his business for profit.

"You don't have to sign in."

Raider turned toward the sweet, melodic voice. His eyes fell

63

on the voluptous form of a dark-haired woman. Her face was round and white, big blue eyes staring back at him. Her lips were parted in a smile. Her breasts strained to burst out of her maroon taffeta dress. Heavy perfume wafted from her toward Raider.

She extended her hand. "You must be the Pinkerton that Adrian sent for."

Raider nodded, taking off his hat. "Yes, ma'am."

Her smile was friendly. "Come, come, no need to be so formal. My name is Helen Mallory. I'm Mr. Thornton's personal secretary."

She touched her black hair, which was done up in a pretty twist. Curls spilled to both sides of her face. It took all of Raider's willpower to keep from staring at her. He had not expected such a lovely flower in the barren heat of Adobe Sands.

"Pleased to make your acquaintance, Miss Mallory."

An expression of pleasant surprise spread over her face. "Why, sir, do I take it that you are a gentleman?"

Raider shrugged. "Well, I used to have this partner who was a dandified sort. I reckon some of it rubbed off on me. Specially when I see a woman who . . . I mean, a lady like yourself."

"And what do they call you, sir?"

"Raider."

She gestured toward a narrow corridor. "Follow me, Mr. Raider."

When she turned, he saw the backside was as well-developed as the front. She sashayed down the hallway with Raider close behind. She directed him into a fancy parlor that undoubtedly bore a woman's touch. Brocade sofas, tea tables, maroon curtains, oriental rugs, doilies.

"Wait here," she told him.

After she had exited, Raider stood motionless in the parlor. He was afraid to sit down or touch anything for fear that his trail dust might soil the ornate furnishings. He studied the pictures on the walls, trying to find anything that would give him a clue as to the disposition of his host and current employer.

"Good afternoon, sir. I see that you are a lover of fine art."

Raider turned back to see a dapper gentleman standing at

the threshold of the parlor. He wore a light-colored tricot suit, a starched shirt, and a silk tie and vest. For a second, Raider thought the sandy-haired man was his old partner, Doc Weatherbee. The resemblance was striking, except for the gentleman's beady brown eyes.

Ace Clanton stood behind the short gentleman, gaping over his shoulder. "I told you he was a big 'un, Mr. Thornton."

"That will be all, Ace," Thornton said curtly.

Clanton gawked at Raider. "You sure you want to—"

"That will be all!" Thornton insisted, never taking his eyes off Raider.

Clanton slunk away, no doubt wondering about his status now that Raider had arrived.

Thornton moved into the room, extending his hand. "Adrian Thornton. They tell me you're called Raider."

The big Pinkerton nodded· "Yes, sir."

He took Thornton's hand. His palm was as soft as a lily. Thornton had never done a day of hard labor in his life.

Thornton offered him a wooden chair. "Go ahead and sit down. Don't worry about the dust. Helen needs something to do around here. She gets bored in Adobe Sands, and, quite frankly, so do I."

Raider eased down in the wooden chair, gazing up at Thornton. "If it's so godforsaken, why do you stay here?"

Thornton smiled, his thin lips parting over white teeth. "I see that you are direct. Good. I like a man who speaks his mind." He started to pace back and forth over the thick rug. "Why do I stay here? As you may be able to tell, Adobe Sands is on its last legs. There's nothing here to keep the homesteaders in the area. They've found the land to be poor for farming and for raising livestock. Naturally I've offered them all a fair price for their land. Many of them have chosen to sell."

Raider's brow was fretted, his eyes narrow.

Thornton kept his smile. "Why am I buying up their land? Some say it's because I'm crazy. What can I gain from a sandy plot of ground where nothing will survive beyond the Gila monsters and the desert snakes? What do you think, Mr. Raider?"

The big man shrugged. "Got to be either one of two things—

gold or the railroad. Why else would a man speculate?''

Thornton nodded his approval. "Very good. You hit the nail directly. With the railroad, I mean. There certainly isn't any gold about. Not even on the California side.''

Raider grimaced. "I don't want to bad-mouth your business here, Mr. Thornton, but the railroad is way north of here.''

Thornton nodded. "The Union Pacific, yes. But do you really believe that will be the only railroad to come this way? Why, there'll be a hundred routes coming west by the turn of the century.''

The big man shrugged. "I reckon you're young enough to wait twenty years for your bet to pay off.''

"Not just me," Thornton replied. "I represent a group of men in Phoenix. We're doing our best to make sure that the railroads will have clear passage through Arizona. That's why we brought you in, sir. To make sure that our interests are best served.''

Raider bristled a little and stood up. "Mr. Thornton . . .''

"Call me Adrian.''

"All right. Adrian." Raider couldn't say that he liked the sound of such a sissy-like name. "I just want one thing clear before we get started. I ain't like Clanton there. Don't think of me as another hired gun that's here to bully sodbusters. I'm a detective. I solve things. Understood?''

Thornton patted his shoulder. "I wouldn't have it any other way. As for that disturbance with the farmer, I've reprimanded Ace about that. He had no right to treat that man in such a manner. In fact, I'm glad I found out about the incident. It will not happen again, I can assure you.''

Raider nodded, sitting down again in the wooden chair. "Okay, now that we got that settled, why don't you tell me what kind of problem you got here in Adobe Sands?''

Thornton poised himself for the explanation, only to be interrupted by a light knocking at the door. Helen Mallory admitted herself without being asked to come in. She carried a silver tray with a teapot, three cups, silver spoons, a creamer, and a bowl of sugar.

"I thought you gentleman might like a nice cup of tea," she

said with a sidelong glance to Raider. "Do you take one lump or two, Mr. Raider?"

The big man squirmed in the seat, not quite sure how to react to Helen's overly attentive eyes.

Thornton sighed impatiently. "For God's sake, Helen, it's a hundred degrees in the shade. Hot tea isn't what we need."

She ignored his disrespectful tone, pouring the tea into the cups. "Don't think I haven't felt this heat. Why, it's simply horrid. Here, Mr. Raider, try this."

He took the cup from her delicate hands and sipped politely. "That's whiskley," he said. "Good whiskey."

She grinned, handing a cup to Thornton. "The finest bourbon from Adrian's private stock." After pouring herself a cup, she sat down on the sofa opposite Raider, keeping her eyes on him. "Don't mind me, gentlemen, keep talking.

Thornton set his cup on the tray. "Helen, please. Raider and I are conducting business here. I don't want you in the way."

For the first time since Raider had met her, Helen Mallory's eyes showed a harsh quality. She glared at Thornton, her lips drawn up in a hateful pout. "I never get to do anything around here!" she squawked. "You're always telling me to leave just when things get interesting."

Thornton took her hand, urging her off the sofa. "Helen, I don't have any time or patience for your tantrums today. If you'd just leave, I'll see you later, at dinner."

She glided to the door with a grace that Raider had seldom seen in women he dealt with. She turned coquettishly, looking back with the soft eyes that had greeted the big man upon his arrival. "Well, Mr. Raider, I do hope that you aren't the kind of man who treats a lady like a common servant girl. I expect you'll join us for dinner."

Raider nodded. "Yes'm."

She smiled broadly and closed the door behind her.

Raider exhaled, casting a quick glance at Thornton.

Thornton waved him off. "Pay her no mind. Women are like cats. They get bored if there are no mice to chase. Then they expect their men to keep them entertained."

"I s'pose," Raider replied, happy to abandon the topic of Helen Mallory. "You were tellin' me about the situation here in Adobe Sands."

Thornton sighed. "Where to begin? As I told you, I've been buying up this worthless land, offering a price comparable to the money paid by the homesteaders when they bought it in the first place."

"That'd be about fifteen cents an acre," Raider offered.

Thornton threw up his hands. "I'm paying them twenty! Some of them jumped at the chance, but several stubborn families refuse to give up."

Raider frowned at his host. "You ain't done nothin' to try to make them leave, have you?"

Thornton laughed. "Of course not. Why the devil would I want to run them off their miserable land? I have enough acreage to meet our purposes. I'm doing them a favor by offering top price for plots that won't even feed a desert fox. They should jump at the chance."

Raider leaned back in the chair, extending his long legs. "Then what's the beef? If you've got what you need and the others aren't in the way, then things should be straight."

Thornton raised an eyebrow. "Then you haven't been told?"

"About what?"

"The priest," Thornton replied. "The padre who has been causing all of the trouble."

Raider squinted at his boots. "Seems I recall Clanton said somethin' about a murderin' padre. That the same one?"

"Father Amerigo Pedroza," Thornton said with a certain note of contempt in his voice. "The champion of the downtrodden. While I try to give the homesteaders a new start with good money for bad land, he whips them up with sermons designed to turn them against me."

Raider thought about it for a moment and then said, "You're tellin' me that a man of God has been killin' people?"

Thornton held up a soft hand, his fingers outstretched. "Five of my men to date. Shot them down in cold blood."

"Didn't even face them head on?" Raider asked.

"Cold blood."

"And you're sure it was the preacher?"

"Every time one of my men died, the padre's cassock was seen flying in the breeze as he escaped." Thornton turned away, looking out of the window. "He's in hiding now. The homesteaders keep him hidden in the hills. My men have searched for weeks now, but we can't seem to find him. I'll be the first to tell you that I'm not a religious sort, Raider, but I can't see how a man of God can wield a six-gun against a man who's trying to help his congregation."

Raider shrugged, his hands folded across his chest. "Maybe he don't want to lose the money in the collection plate."

Thornton spun around, his face showing a pleased expression at Raider's comment. "I'd never thought of that. Yes, I see what you mean."

"On the other side of the saddle, maybe he's just plain loco," the big man offered. "And you're sure it's the priest?"

"His face is always shaded by the hood of his cassock," Thornton replied, "but it's him, no matter how much he tries to hide it."

Raider considered his next question, thinking at first that it was sort of stupid, but then deciding to ask it anyway. "What's a cassock?"

Thornton explained that it was a hooded garment, like a robe, that was worn by priest, friars, and brothers. "There's something else, too," he said.

Raider watched as Thornton removed something from a desk on the other side of the room. He dropped a small sack in the big man's lap. Raider opened the sack and poured the contents into his hand. He studied the feathered trinkets and carved bones.

"Do you have any idea what these are?" Thornton asked.

"Maybe," Raider replied. "Where'd you get them?"

"There are five of them," Thornton said. "One for each man who has died. Clanton found them on all five bodies."

Raider held up one of the charms, scrutinizing it in the afternoon light. The shape had been tied with horsehair, fashioned to resemble a small man. The carved bones were in the form of rattlesnake heads.

"Apache," Raider said. "Mescalero Apache."

Thornton gave a nervous, involuntary laugh. "Indians?"

Raider nodded. "But not like the kind we're used to seein' out here. They're like priests themselves, shamans, witch doctors, big medicine. They worship the forces of nature—wind, water, fire, animals." He lifted the snake head. "Snakes are just one of their gods."

"Extraordinary!" Thornton exclaimed.

"Maybe. Dangerous too. This stuff is their way of puttin' the whammy on anybody that's doin' 'em wrong. You had any run-ins with Injuns?"

Thornton shook off the suggestion. "Never. I can't say that I've ever seen an Apache before."

Raider smiled. "Well, that don't mean they haven't seen you."

Thornton's face registered his concern. "You don't think . . ."

"I don't know what to think just yet. I been in town for about two hours, and so far I had me a fight and been shown some scary medicine that I ain't seen for years."

"Why so scary?" asked the serious host.

Raider shifted in the chair, looking down at the sack of trinkets. "Next to Comanche, Apaches are the most dangerous Injuns you'd ever want to run across. Mescaleros are mean. Some of them are half Mexican. They'll load up on peyote cactus and do strange things. Back when I was a pup, I seen a Mescalero walk across a firebed without burnin' his feet. That old boy kept a pet rattlesnake in his cave. Claimed he slept with it."

"You don't expect me to believe that," Thornton said, half smiling.

Raider stood up. "I don't rightly care what you believe, Mr. Thornton. I just want you to know what's goin' on here. Which leads me to this. If your preacher is leavin' these things around, he's pretty much playin' with a fifty-one-card deck. I seen religious men before. No preacher I ever met would cotton to Injun magic. They all believe in the Bible, and as far as I know, it don't say nothin' in there about worshipin' rattlesnakes."

A shudder played through Thornton's body. He hadn't counted on the unknown factor, something Raider had learned to live with during his years as a Pinkerton. Things weren't always what they seemed, even when you had the flat-out evidence right in front of you.

"You mind if I keep these trinkets, Mr. Thornton? They might help me when I start to poke around."

Thornton smiled encouragingly. "Poke at will, Raider. I want you to get to the bottom of this thing as quickly as you can. This sort of affair discourages investors, if you know what I mean."

Raider nodded, even though Thornton's financial interests were not his main worry. "I want you to round up any of your men who saw this padre while he was shootin'. Get one who can write and have him lay out all the details. Make 'em tell everything, the who and what, where it happened, all of it."

Thornton had a contented look on his face. "I can see that you Pinkertons are as professional as your reputation claims."

"Sometimes stuff'll get by me, but in the end there ain't much that I miss. Now if you'll excuse me, I'll be findin' a place to bunk for the night."

"Nonsense!" Thornton replied. "I've an empty hotel here. You can pick your own room. All of your meals will be provided. Anything you need. You have only to ask."

"Much obliged. I reckon it beats sleepin' in the livery."

Thornton ushered Raider out of the parlor and down the corridor to the front desk. The dapper land baron slipped around behind the desk and pulled one of the keys out of the slot on the wall. "Room thirteen."

Raider frowned. "I'm kinda superstitious, if you don't mind."

"Very well," Thornton replied. "Take eleven. That's a lucky number for a lot of people. The room faces the street too."

Raider put the key in his vest pocket. "I'm gonna check on my horse at the stable. I'll be back shortly. Is there a key to the front door?"

"It's never locked. Come and go at will. If you miss dinner, you can find yourself something in the kitchen."

Raider tipped his hat and started for the door.

"Welcome aboard," Thornton said. "I feel much safer with you here."

"Don't forget that list," Raider offered. "I need to know

what ever'body saw. It'll help me a heap.''

Thornton nodded, smiling. "Good luck to you.''

Raider pushed out into the street. The sun was dropping, even though the heat had not abated any. He glanced toward the saloon and the livery. The street was empty. Where had the spectators gone?

He tried the livery first. The stallion was in a stall, freshly rubbed down and munching oats. The blacksmith hovered over his anvil, banging with a heavy hammer on red-hot iron. Raider tried to ask him questions about the padre and the situation with the homesteaders.

"Don't have nothin' to say,'' was the reluctant reply.

Raider asked the man how he felt about Adrian Thornton.

The smithy gave a look from the corners of his eyes. "Mister, I wouldn't have no business at all if it weren't for Mr. Thornton. He keeps me open. If it wasn't for him, I'd be out of this town.''

"What about the man with the harness-bred?''

"The one you fought for? I don't know a thing about that. You'd have to ask the dad-blamed sodbuster himself. If you can find him.''

"Why'd he light out like that?'' Raider asked.

The smithy turned his back to the big man. "I got work to do, pardner. Your black done broke a shoe. If you want it fixed, you'd best leave me be.''

He went back to pounding the red iron.

Raider decided to try the saloon. When he pushed through the swinging doors he was greeted by emptiness. All of the men who had witnessed the fight were long gone. The bartender raised up, no doubt hoping the big man would toss more money his way.

"Don't look like anybody wants to drink with me,'' Raider said.

The bartender shrugged, filling a shot glass. "Nope, they all done hightailed it after they seen you drinkin' with Clanton.''

Raider eased to up the the bar and sipped at the whiskey. He didn't want to get drunk. He needed a clear head if he was going to unmask the mysterious padre—if it was a padre.

He eyed the bartender. "I'm gonna ask you straight out,

pardner. What the hell is goin' on in this town?''

''Depends on who you ask,'' the bartender replied with a sly smile.

''I'm askin' you.''

The bartender gestured around him. ''This ain't my place, but I treat it like it is. Thornton set me up here. Bought this dive from my former boss and left me to run it.''

''What happened to your boss?''

''Took off like the rest of 'em.''

''Why?''

''Look around you, big man. Would you stay in this hellhole? Ain't much here for a man who's lookin' to make a livin'. I got me a Mexican girl upstairs, and Thornton pays me good, otherwise I'd be out of here faster'n pullin' a greasy string out of a coyote's ass.''

Raider drained the shot glass and asked for a drink of water. When his throat was wet, he regarded the barkeeper again. ''What's this I hear about a padre killin' people?''

Narrow eyes on the man's face. ''You some kind of law or somethin'?''

''Thornton brought me in to help straighten things out. Said he's been payin' a fair price for worthless land. Ever'thing legal-like. I ain't rightly the law, but I'm close. Pinkerton by trade.''

The bartender sighed and poured himself a shot. He drank and slammed the glass down. ''I got to be straight with you, big feller. I don't know what the hell is goin' on around here. Yeah, I can tell you that Thornton is payin' top dollar for land that ain't that great.'' He drew a line in the dust on the bar. ''Here's the Little Sands River. There's some farmland on both sides. I don't know that anybody ever got anything to grow there. Some had sheep, others tried cows and horses. I seen 'em come and go.''

Raider tipped back his Stetson, exhaling. ''Anybody puttin' pressure on them sodbusters to move out when they ain't wantin' to?''

''Can't say as I know.''

Raider scowled at the man. ''Can't say? Or won't?''

"Go ask them sodbusters."

"I plan to," Raider replied. "What about that padre? You know anythin' about him?"

The bartender looked out toward the street. "Used to have a nice little church here before the padre went crazy and burned it down. Used to have whites, Mexicans, and Indians alike, all prayin' at the same altar. Then the padre went loco and started shootin' ever'body."

"And you seen him shoot people?" Raider asked.

"I ain't. Others have. You'll just have to find 'em and ask 'em."

Raider slammed two bits on the table. "I reckon I will."

He turned and started for the door.

"Big 'un," the bartender called.

Raider wheeled back.

"I'm just one man," the bartender said. "I got to look after myself, you know what I mean? I can't be mixed up in anything that don't concern me. But I wish you luck."

Raider left without a reply, heading back for the hotel. He paused at the front door, glancing at the leveled ruins of the church at the other end of the street. Had the priest really burned it to the ground? What kind of loco preacher would destroy his own church? There were a hell of a lot of questions to answer.

Raider pushed through the door, into the cool shadows of the lobby. No one greeted him, so he headed upstairs. The room was open. His hand strayed down to his Colt before he walked in.

The bed had been made, and there was a fresh pitcher of water on the nightstand. Raider smelled the perfume in the air. Helen Mallory had been there. Her soft hands had turned down the bedsheets.

There was a note on the pillow. "Dinner is at six. Helen." Just thinking about her sent the need coursing through his body. But he had to stay away from her. Maybe he'd skip dinner.

He moved to the window, peering out at the burnt ruins of the church, silently thanking Titus Tilden for giving him another impossible case. How the hell was he going to draw down on a padre? He turned away, unbuckling his gunbelt. Maybe it wouldn't come to shooting. Maybe he could take the padre alive. Still, if it came to six-guns, he might just have to find it in him to send the preacher straight to his Maker.

As he turned back into the room, something on the mirror caught his eye. An envelope had been stuck between the glass and the wood frame. Raider opened it and looked at the hand-written report on the encounters between the padre and Thornton's men. Raider had to hand it to Thornton, he certainly worked fast.

The big man leaned back on the bed and began to read the eyewitness accounts of the six-gun priest.

CHAPTER EIGHT

By the time Raider had finished reading the handwritten reports, the sun had disappeared from the sky. He got up off the bed and lit an oil lamp to brighten the room. As the flame swelled from the wick, he sat on the edge of the bed, considering what he had just read.

The accounts of the pistol-wielding priest were remarkably the same. Both times the padre had appeared to attack several of Thornton's men who were in the process of making "offers" to the local homesteaders. According to Thornton's men, they were acting peaceably, thereby making the attacks unprovoked. But why would the padre force a showdown when there was no need for one? Maybe he was just crazy.

Raider leaned back on the bed, peering up at the reflection from the lamp as it danced on the ceiling. There were a few other things to consider. He thought about the barkeeper and the liveryman, how both of them were loyal to Adrian Thornton. Both had been reluctant to offer information about their boss man. Then there was Thornton himself. What if he had been lying about the pressure brought to bear on the homesteaders? Raider had seen Clanton bullying the man who had left town.

But if Thornton did plan to force out the homesteaders, why had he brought in Raider? Wouldn't he have been eager to run them off without any authority present to witness his treachery? On the surface, Thornton seemed like nothing more than a careless businessman. He had even been penitent about Clanton's roughing up the sodbuster.

Raider sighed deeply. He considered the bizarre accounts of

the pistol-packing father. Thornton's men described the priest's accuracy with a Colt. He had killed all five men with five shots, shooting quickly and then escaping to the sanctuary of the hills. Despite all their searching, Thornton's men had not been able to find him.

Another thing bothered the big Pinkerton from Arkansas. Why did Thornton have a gang of men in the first place? What was he afraid of losing?

Someone rapped on the door.

Raider sat up, reaching for his Colt on the bedpost. "Yeah?"

"Dinner, big man."

It was Ace Clanton. Raider got up and let him in. Clanton carried a supper tray full of food.

"Mr. Thornton sent me up with this when you didn't show for dinner," Clanton said.

Raider took the tray from him. "Thanks, Ace. You mind hangin' around here for a few minutes?"

Clanton shrugged. "No, I don't mind. I could come back later, though, if you want to eat in peace. Miss Helen whomped up some good vittles. Deer meat, potatoes, beans, and gravy. Got some cornbread in there too."

Raider had to admit that it smelled good. He sat down on the bed and started to eat. Clanton hung by the door, watching him.

"Tell me somethin', Ace," Raider said, his jaw grinding. "Has Thornton ever ordered you to make a homesteader give up his land?"

Clanton laughed. "Nosiree," he replied. "Mr. Thornton don't believe in that. He said he's got plenty of land now. He don't care if them homesteaders rot in their sod huts."

Raider nodded. "What about this priest? You ever see him shoot?"

The brown-lipped man eyed the big Pinkerton. "Why you ask that?"

"Preachers ain't usually good with guns," Raider replied. "According to your boys, this padre is a regular shootist. Cut them down like they were tin cans on a rail fence."

Clanton rubbed his chin. "Never thought about it before. I reckon a preacher wouldn't be such a good shot. But hell, big man, this one is. I seen him with my own eyes. Plugged five of my best boys.''

Raider looked up at Clanton. "How many men you got here, Ace?''

"About a dozen now," Clanton replied. "Got 'em stayin' in a bunkhouse out on the edge of town. Why? You need a hand?''

"No." Raider went back to the venison. "I just wondered why Thornton feels like he needs so much firepower. What's he afraid of?''

Thornton's ramrod had a peculiar glint in his eyes as he considered the question. Finally he replied, "I reckon he's afraid of losin' what he has, big 'un. Tough parts hereabouts. Never know who's gonna come along and try to take ever'thin' away from you.

Raider nodded, swallowing a mouthful. "Well," he offered, "I guess the only thing to do is talk to some of the homesteaders hereabouts. I've heard every side of the story except theirs.'' He lifted his eyes to catch Clanton's reaction.

The man with the scar on his cheek stayed cool, disinterested. "Ain't but one big spread left. That'd be the Calders out near Little Sands River. I can show you the shortcut way to go. I'll ride out with you.''

"No need," Raider replied. "I'll find it.''

Clanton squinted at him. "Rough parts, big man. Even for somebody as quick as you.''

"I'll take that chance.''

Clanton hesitated, not knowing whether to stay or go.

Raider grinned at him. "Don't worry, Ace. If I need you, you'll be the first to know.''

"Suit yourself.''

Clanton slipped out and closed the door behind him.

Raider finished his supper, using the cornbread to sop up the rest of the gravy. The meal satisfied his hunger, but he still had a bee buzzing around inside his head. Of all the strange goings-on, the one thing that bothered him most was the appearance of the Mescalero charms near all the dead bodies. If the preacher was shooting and running, how did he manage to plant the Indian trinkets?

He recalled the words of the bartender: "Used to have whites, Mexicans, and Indians alike, all prayin' at the same altar."

Maybe there was some real connection between the padre and the Mescaleros. Or maybe someone was lying to make things more confusing. Of course, if the priest had laid an ambush, he could have planted the trinkets ahead of time. Raider had that antsy feeling he got during a case sometimes. He wanted to get moving, to continue asking questions.

Another knock at the door. Had Clanton come back? Raider hoped so. He wanted to ask him about the Mescalero charms.

"Come on in, Ace."

The perfume hit him as soon as the door cracked open. It sure as hell wasn't Ace Clanton who slipped into the room. Helen Mallory closed the door behind her. She wore a fancy black dress that showed off the shaded canyon of her bosom.

"How was supper?" she asked, smiling deviously.

Raider nodded, trying not to direct too much attention toward her healthy cleavage. "It filled up the wormholes in my belly."

She laughed. "You are a caution, Mr. Raider. I'd say that you must hail from north Texas."

He shook his head. "Arkansas. Judgin' by your cookin', Miss Mallory, I'd say you come from Tennessee."

"Kentucky," she replied. "We were both close."

The look in her eyes told him that she wouldn't mind getting a little closer. Raider wasn't the kind of man who jumped on his host's ladyfriend. Even though Thornton wasn't married to her and the secretary bit was a ruse, Raider still figured it was bad form to spark anything with the buxom woman. He wanted to ask her a few questions, however.

"Why don't you open that door?" he asked.

She grinned, her lips parted in a coy pout. "Are you afraid of me, Raider?"

"No. I just don't want Mr. Thornton gettin' the wrong idea."

She shrugged. "He won't. In fact, he sent me up here to see if there's anything I can do for you." She moved closer to the bed. "Is there anything I can do for you?"

Raider stood up, inching away from her, backing toward the window. "As a matter of fact, there is somethin' you can do."

She pressed her body against his, pinning him to the casement. Her hands ran over his chest. "You name it, cowboy."

Raider gently pushed her away. "I want you to answer some questions for me."

Her eyes betrayed her disappointment. She turned, giving him the cold shoulder. "Questions? Sure. Why not?" Spinning back toward him. "Ask me anything. I'm not afraid to tell the truth. I—"

She screamed.

The window shattered next to Raider's head. Glass flew everywhere. Raider dived for the floor, taking Helen with him.

"What's going on?" she cried.

"Somebody tryin' to make sure I don't stay alive too long."

The rifle chattered again, fire streaming from the muzzle in the darkness. Raider grabbed his Peacemaker and crawled to the window. He raised his head, only to have the rifle kick up splinters on the windowsill.

"The light," he whispered. "Turn it down."

Helen reached for the oil lamp, but the rifle beat her to the punch. A slug shattered the glass, sending pools of flame in every direction. Raider and the woman did their best to stamp out the fire before it engulfed the room. Adrian Thornton rushed in to help them.

"What the hell happened?" Thornton cried.

"Stay down," Raider cautioned. "Somebody's shootin' at me from across the street."

Thornton started toward the window. Raider grabbed his employer and pulled him to the floor. "You want to get your ass shot off?"

Thornton's body trembled at the threat. "What are you going to do?"

Raider lifted the Peacemaker, thumbing back the hammer. "I'm gonna go get the son of a bitch who's shootin' at me. Y'all stay low and don't move till I get back. If Clanton shows up, send him out after me."

Thornton scooted next to his personal secretary, putting his arms around her shoulders. "But what if—"

"No buts," Raider replied. "If I don't come back, get to the nearest telegraph and send a message to my agency to send another man in here. You savvy?"

Thornton nodded. The rifle splintered more wood from the casement. Thornton turned white.

"And stay away from that window!" the big man cried.

He didn't have to tell Thornton twice.

The man Allan Pinkerton referred to as his wild card rolled through the door and started out into night to search for the source of the bushwhacking rifle fire.

The full moon was high, giving Raider a good view of the silhouetted structure across the street. The shots had come from the roof of the closed general store. Raider paused in the doorway of the hotel, watching the parapet of the building. A dark, pointed shape moved against the backdrop of the glowing moon.

Raider swung out of the doorway, firing the Colt at the mysterious figure. The rifle chattered a return volley. Raider dived into the street, rolling under the slugs that slammed into the dust.

He came up running toward the general store.

The shots stopped.

Raider pinned himself against the facade of the storefront, listening for sounds of movement above. A pair of boots scraped across the flat roof. Raider swung around the side of the building, stepping slowly through the coolness of the alleyway.

A horse snorted in back of the general store.

Raider eased toward the mount, his Colt cocked and ready.

The horse whinnied again. Raider came toward the edge of the building, only to be met by the rattling of a rifle lever. But he had to get off a shot. He stuck the Peacemaker around the corner and fired blindly.

The rifle answered his burst, urging him back.

Raider dived again, rolling toward a rain barrel on the other side of the alley.

Rifle fire chased him all the way.

He came up behind the rain barrel, firing at the dark shape that leapt from the roof into the saddle. But the assassin was too quick. He fired the repeater from the hip, chopping the stays of the rain barrel with an offering of hot lead.

Raider dropped his head, but not before he got a glimpse of the hooded figure against the pale moon. The assailant was wearing some kind of robe. Just like a priest.

Hooves pounded the dry ground, escaping into the night. Raider came up firing, but he knew he had hit only air as the horse galloped out of sight. He ran back down the alley, rounding the corner and turning for the livery.

"Raider!"

Adrian Thornton called to him from the hotel window.

"I'm gonna follow him," the big man cried. "Stay put till I get back."

But when he got to the livery, the smithy said that his mount wasn't ready yet. The broken shoe wasn't fixed, and it would take at least a half hour for the new shoe to be hammered into place. Raider cursed under his breath and then ran back to the hotel.

Thornton and Helen Mallory were still in his room.

"Did you get him?" Thornton asked, lighting a candle.

Raider shook his head. "He had a horse waiting, and my mount ain't in any shape to run."

Helen peered out the window toward the general store roof. "Who was it? I mean, did you at least see him?"

"I got a glimpse," Raider replied. "He was wearin' one of them cassock things."

Thornton's eyes opened wide. "The padre?"

"That's what I'm guessin'." The big man glared at his new employer. "Funny, me bein' put in a room that overlooks the street. How come, Mr. Thornton? Answer me!"

Thornton shook his head. "You were the one who wanted to change rooms, Raider. I offered you a room in the back."

The big man sighed, lowering his head. "Yeah, that's right. Sorry." He looked out the window. "But that loco preacher knows I'm here. I ain't even been in town for twenty-four hours and he's already shootin' at me."

They heard clomping on the stairs. Raider fell back against the wall, urging Thornton and Helen to do the same. Ace Clanton pushed his head into the room.

"Hey," he called, "what's all the commotion?"

Raider breathed easier. "Just some shootin'."

Clanton stared at the broken windows. "Hell, I knew that. I could hear it all the way down the street. I was on my way back to the bunkhouse when all hell broke loose."

Raider gestured toward the general store. "Looks like the good padre knows I'm here. Tried to pepper me from across the street."

Clanton shook his head. "You believe me now about the preacher?"

"Reckon I do," the big man replied.

Thornton moved nervously toward the hallway. "Well, you can't stay in here tonight. I'll get another room ready downstairs. Helen, give me a hand, will you."

They left together, hurrying to their task.

Clanton's boots crunched in the broken glass. "Didn't take him long to find you."

Raider started to gather up his gear.

Clanton leaned back against the wall. "I tried to tell you to be careful, Raider. Father Pedroza is a bad one. He's plain damned dangerous."

"So am I, Ace. So am I."

He lifted his saddlebags over his shoulder and started downstairs. Clanton followed, offering further admonitions about the padre. Raider half listened, but he did not need any more warnings. The big man from Arkansas knew the preacher from Adobe Sands was playing for keeps.

The new room was fancy, all curtains and fine linen. Raider didn't even notice the difference. He threw his rifle on the bed and pointed a finger at Adrian Thornton, who was turning down the flame on an oil lamp.

"I need answers, Thornton." He threw his saddlebags into a chair. The noise caused the dapper blond-haired gentleman to startle. "How come you got a dozen men to guard you? What is it you need protection from?"

Thornton stepped forward, his beady eyes showing the first signs of anger. "You saw what that madman did!" he cried. "He almost killed us all!"

Raider broke open his Colt and dumped the spent cartridges on the rug. "I was there, Thornton. And I don't blame you for bein' scared of that padre. But somebody around here done somethin' to get things stirred up. Even a crazy man don't fight until provoked. Unless that padre just sold himself over to the devil.''

"Please," Thornton said, backing off, "believe me when I say that I haven't done a thing to warrant these attacks on me and my men. Yes, I do have quite a few hands to assist me, but they all stay at an old bunkhouse on the edge of town. Don't they, Ace?''

Raider was not aware that Clanton had moved into the room behind him.

"They're all on the edge of town," Clanton replied. "And even when Mr. Thornton sent us out to deal with them, to make an offer on the property, we were peaceable.''

Raider scowled at the lanky ramrod. "You lost five men in two trips. Two men came back from one ambush, one from the other. How come you need four men to cut a deal with sodbusters?''

"These people can be ignorant," Thornton offered. "Ace took three men along with him in case things got out of hand on the other side.''

"Somethin' got out of hand," Raider said, "or that padre wouldn't be sprayin' ever'thing in sight.''

Clanton scowled back at Raider. "Look here, Arkansas, if you don't believe we settled peaceable with the homesteaders, you just get the names from Mr. Thornton and go find two or three of 'em. Hell, most of 'em was happy to get back east to their kin. For a lot of 'em it was like bein' staked to their life savin's all over again.''

Thornton's tone was pleading again. "Why do you insist on believing that we have intimidated these people?''

Raider exhaled, reaching for his gunbelt. "I'm just lookin' for answers, Mr. Thornton." He loaded the cylinder of the Peacemaker and then looked at both of them. "Sorry, boys. I just get a little cantankerous when I been shot at. 'Scuse me, if you will.''

Clanton shrugged and nodded. "Yeah, I know the feelin', big 'un.''

"We're all on edge," Thornton added.

Raider slid the Colt into his holster and then buckled the belt around him. "Clanton, see if you can round up a torch.''

Thornton frowned. "Where are you going?"

"On the roof of the general store."

When a torch was procured, all three men crossed the street and went through the alley to the back of the store. The bushwhacker had climbed up a barrel and along a drainpipe. A lower porch roof was easily accessible, and from there they had only to hop onto the flat roof above.

Raider held the torch high overhead, swinging it from side to side.

Clanton stayed back in the shadows. "What the devil are you lookin' for, Raider? Ain't nothin' up here."

"That's where you're wrong, Ace." The torch luffed as he swung the flame low over the planks. "Sometimes a man thinks he ain't leavin' somethin' when he's really paintin' a path to his door."

Thornton, who had had some difficulty on the climb up, stayed to Raider's right, scanning the roof as if his life depended on it. "I don't know what that padre would leave unless it was a . . . what? There. Swing the torch this way. It was shiny."

Raider bent over, almost touching the shiny object with the flame of the torch. "Brass cartridge." He picked it up and examined it more closely. "Winchester. Thirty caliber."

Clanton looked over his shoulder. "Just one? Hell, from what I saw and heard he emptied the whole rifle at you."

Raider nodded. "But he tried to pick them up before he left. Didn't want to leave anything for us to find." He stood up, waving the torch over the parapet. "Unless he left that!"

He had to draw back the flame to keep the feathers from igniting.

Thornton moved forward, lifting the figure into the light. "Just like the trinket I showed you before."

"Mescalero medicine," Raider said.

Clanton looked dubious. "What the hell is a Mescalero?"

"Apache Indian," Thornton replied, proud that the knowledge was his. "Raider told me. They work magic with these charms. You should recognize this charm, Ace. It's just like the others you brought in."

Raider turned to the scar-faced ramrod. "You found the charms near the dead bodies?"

Clanton nodded. "Yeah."

"Where'd they come from?" Raider asked.

"I don't know," Clanton replied. "They were just layin' there. When I saw 'em, I thought I ought to bring 'em to Mr. Thornton."

Raider used the torch again. "The mate ought to be here with it."

They looked for a few more minutes until they found the carved bone.

Thornton held up the figurine. "It looks like a coyote head."

"Warnin' us to stay away," Raider said. "The coyote will pick our bones if we don't."

A warm wind picked up from the west, stirring the dust on the rooftop. Raider turned, peering straight into the hot breeze. He could see the hills against the moon, insignificant bumps in the distance.

"The padre rode that way," he said, pointing toward the mountains.

Clanton stepped up beside him. "He could be hidin' anywhere up there. Lots of caves and ledges. A few mountain lions too. I reckon that old boy is gonna be as hard to find as a cougar."

Raider turned away from the pitted blast of the wind. "I'll track him down. If he's there, I'll find him."

Thornton started for the way down. "I'm going back to check on Helen. You gentlemen can come along if you like."

Clanton went after his boss.

Raider stopped him. "Ace, how do I get out to that place you told me about? The Calders, wasn't it?"

Clanton pointed toward the moon. "Straight on out. Like you're goin' to the hills. Five miles or so."

Raider just nodded. He handed Clanton the torch to light their path down. When they were gone, the big man turned toward the street, watching as Thornton went back into the hotel and Clanton mounted up to ride to the bunkhouse on the edge of town. Raider had decided to visit the bunkhouse himself, after he paid a visit to the homesteaders and had a look through the hills in search of the preacher.

The town looked sort of sad in the moonlight. Adobe Sands

wasn't dead, but the vultures were hovering overhead. Still, for a town on its last legs, it had been anything but dull for Allan Pinkerton's toughest operative.

"Hey! Lawman!"

The voice had come from the street.

Raider lifted the Colt halfway, until he saw the liveryman waving at him. He dropped the Peacemaker and leaned on the parapet. "What the devil do you want, smith?"

"I done got your horse ready," the man replied. "He's there anytime you want him."

Raider thanked him and promised him an extra half dollar when he paid his bill. The smithy replied that Mr. Thornton was taking care of everything. He turned and started back to the stable.

Raider decided it was time to get down. He had enough moonlight to find the handholds. Before he climbed off, he peered to the west. The hills were dark and threatening. The padre could be hiding anywhere in there.

The wind kicked up again, stirring clouds of dust that swirled over the white, lonely circle of the moon.

CHAPTER NINE

When Raider got back to his room, the bedcovers had been turned down and the heavy scent of Helen Mallory's perfume hung in the warm air. Raider cracked a window, hoping that the maddening smell would waft itself into the night wind. If she was trying to drive him crazy, she was doing a damned good job of it.

He took off his boots and his gunbelt and reclined on the feather mattress. How the hell had Adobe Sands ever supported such a fancy place? Had it really been a town where sodbusters planted their hopes and harvested grief? How did the bushwhacking padre fill his church in the heyday of the soon-to-be ghost town?

Despite his employer's speculative designs on the area, Raider could not help but feel that Adobe Sands had one foot in the grave already. Sure, the railroad might come through—someday. But Adobe Sands would be dust on the plain by that time.

He fluffed the pillow and buried his head in it, trying to close his eyes. But his head wasn't ready to quit for the evening. He rolled over and looked into the darkness of the ceiling.

What did the padre think he was fighting for? If Thornton had been aboveboard with all his dealings, then the homesteaders hadn't been slighted. They didn't need a protector. Maybe it was something else, a personal grudge against Thornton. Why else would the padre try to kill Raider, a man who had come in search of the truth?

Raider needed to know more about Thornton. He knew the

89

way to do it, too. Another reason he could not sleep—Helen Mallory. The sight of her had bothered him from the first minute he saw her. And when she had pressed her body against him, he had had to catch his breath.

He'd talk to her later.

The damned night was hot. He got up and undressed to his skivvies. Again he put his head on the pillow, reaching back one time to make sure he could find his Colt in the dark. The Peacemaker was the most dependable thing in the big man's life. It had never let him down.

Tossing and turning, he tried to get comfortable in the soft bed. Usually a feather mattress knocked him right out. He listened to the wind and the creaking of the hotel. There were a lot of noises in the night. Including the soft shuffling of feet in the hallway.

Raider sat up, grabbing his pistol. The slippered footfalls halted by his door. He started to thumb back the hammer of the Colt, but then he caught the scent on the breeze. He dropped the gun in the holster and leaned back with his hands behind his head.

"It's open, Miss Mallory," he said in a low voice.

She came through the door in a flowing white nightgown. "I just wanted to see if I could do anything for you before I went to bed. Perhaps I should light this lamp. . . ."

"Leave it," the big man replied. "I'm glad you came. But what we have to do, we can do in the dark."

She laughed. "I like you, Raider. You don't beat around the bush. Here, let me rub your shoulders."

Raider drew the bedcovers over his body. "That ain't what I had in mind. You just stay over there by the door."

He detected a note of frustration in her sigh. "Adrian is sound asleep," she replied. "And he don't care about me anyway. We've been together now for five years. I know we ain't married, but I don't care. And I don't think Adrian can make a baby. We've done it times when I told him it was safe, only it wasn't. But I never got in the family way. I don't know if he would have married me if I had. A man takes a woman for granted after he's been with her for a while. Have you ever been with a woman for a long time, Raider?"

He shrugged. "No. But that's the way I like it. Go on, Helen. Keep talkin' about Adrian. Where'd you meet him?"

Even though he could not clearly see her face, he figured she was smiling. A short laugh escaped from her lips. Her nightgown rustled a little as she moved toward the bed. He felt her weight on the mattress as she sat down. Then her hand slid under the covers to touch his leg.

"You want something from me," she said. "I want something from you. You'll get what you want when I get what I want. Savvy?"

His skin prickled under her soft hand. "Helen, what if Thornton comes in here and catches us?"

A deep, melodic sigh from her throat. "I don't know. I suppose you could kill him."

"Helen!"

"Oh, he's snoring. He never wakes up, believe me, I know. A couple of hot nights I tried to get him to rise and shine. You know what it's like to lie in bed on a hot night, your body aching?"

Raider fought hard to catch his breath. "Yeah. I know."

"An even trade," she said, rubbing his thigh. "What I want for what you want. Deal?"

The wind blew sand against the window. Raider felt the heat of the bedcovers on his torso. He threw them off.

"It's a deal, lady. What the hell do you want?"

"Lie down on your stomach."

"What?"

"Just do it," she insisted.

When Raider was prone on the mattress, her soft hands reached for the muscles of his shoulderrs. She began to knead the knotted sinews like bread dough. Raider tensed at first, but as she worked on him, he felt the knots unwinding. The massage began to relax him.

"You're all keyed up," she said. "I reckon it must be something to get shot at all the time."

Raider grunted. Her hands went down his back to the base of his spine. She seemed to find every sore spot on his body.

"I learned this in Tennessee," she murmured. "I used to work in a house where gentlemen came for relaxation. I hope that doesn't make you think ill of me, Mr. Raider.''

''Some of my best friends work in them kind of places,'' he replied.

''I met Adrian in Memphis,'' she said. ''He's from Connecticut originally. Came to Tennessee right before I met him. Used to deal cards in the house where I worked. He was . . .''

She stopped. Her hands stopped too. Did he hear heavy breathing?

''Go on,'' Raider urged. ''Keep talkin'.''

''No.'' She patted his fanny. ''Turn over. I want to rub your front.''

There was nothing to do but obey her.

When he was on his back, her hands stripped away his undershorts. She wasted no time grabbing his cock. Her masssage had taken him halfway, now her fingers did the rest. He stiffened under her touch.

Her voice had a breathless quality. ''My word, I've seen my share of peckers, but this one . . .''

She put her mouth on him, rolling the head of his prick between her lips. Raider's legs went weak. She started up and down, taking him in and out. Her fingers worked on his scrotum, intensifying the sensation.

Raider opened and closed his fists. The urge to get on top of her was overwhelming. He didn't know how much longer he would last inside her mouth. Helen kept up her oral ministrations, torturing him to the point of climax, withdrawing right before his sap started to rise.

She stood up, lifting the nightgown over her head. He could see her large breasts in the glow of the moon. She slid down next to him, stretching out, rubbing her hands over his hairy chest.

Raider immediately cupped her breasts, rubbing her erect nipples. ''You're a damned fine woman, Helen.''

She guided his fingers to her wet crotch. Raider slipped a fingertip through the folds of her cunt, searching for the sensitive area that always drove women wild. He didn't know the name for it, but he sure as hell knew that it got them going.

Helen's body shivered. Her legs tightened and she squirmed into him. Her hands kept tugging at his manhood.

"You know a lot about women," she whispered, her tongue rolling on the outside of her mouth. "Kiss my tits."

She rolled over on her back. Raider rubbed her as he lowered his mouth to her nipples. Helen emitted little moans. Raider nursed like a baby, growing more impatient to be inside her.

"I'm gonna put it in," he whispered.

Her hand touched his shoulder. "Remember," she teased, "it's what I want." She pushed him down on his back.

Raider didn't see the sense in fighting her. He wanted her ready to answer questions. Besides, he was having one of the best times he had ever known with a lady. Helen had a flare for treating a man right.

"How come women always want to be on top?" he muttered.

She giggled, running her hands along the tight plateau of his stomach. "We want to see what it's like," she replied. "Don't worry. You can be on top later. We've got all night. You aren't sleepy, are you?"

"No. I sure as hell ain't sleepy."

She got up on her knees, straddling his crotch. Raider reached for her breasts, cupping them in his palms. Helen took his cock in hand, aligning the stiff flesh with the entrance of her cunt.

She grunted a little as the head of Raider's cock entered her. He thrust his hips upward, trying to drive it in further. She sat down all the way, impaling herself on him.

"Damn, that feels good," she said in a voice that reverberated through the room.

"Shh," Raider said, a finger to his lips.

They hesitated, lying there locked together. Both of them listened to the creaking of the boards in the hallway. Was it Thornton, risen from his bed? Or just a draft of wind rushing through the corridor?

"He's snoring," Helen said. "Listen."

Sure enough, Raider could hear the droning roar of a man fast asleep.

Helen resumed her motion, bouncing off him, rising and falling. She knew exactly what she was doing. As her hot releases came one after another, she drove him toward his own inevitable climax.

He reached for her backside, gripping her plump buttocks.

"No," he whispered. "Not yet."

"What's wrong with you?"

"Nothin'." He rolled her off him. "I just want it my way for a while."

She giggled. "What are you gonna do? Put it in my bum? Or take me like a bitch in heat?"

He parted her thighs, moving to climb on top of her. "Nothin' wild," he said. "Just old-fashioned fuckin'."

She spread her legs and lifted them toward the ceiling. Raider prodded her crotch until he felt the wetness on the dull point of his prick. Her head fell back, her mouth gasping for air.

Raider penetrated the soft folds of her cunt, delivering his half of the bargain. Their bodies were like one, moving together as if they had been bed partners for years. Helen cried out so loudly that Raider was afraid Thornton might hear her. But he could not stop himself. He forced the smile from her face, turning it into the anguished expression of ecstasy.

"Inside me," she whispered, biting his ear. "Deep inside me."

Again he obeyed her, collapsing as his prick exploded. He buried himself as deeply as he could go, prompting a deeper release from the woman underneath him. Helen twitched, keeping him trapped inside.

"More," she insisted.

Raider kissed her lips.

"Don't stop, Raider."

He rolled off anyway.

"You got to answer questions for me," he said. "Unless you plan to welsh on our bargain."

She sighed, and he imagined that she would pout for a while.

"You aren't very romantic," she accused.

Raider chuckled. "No, I guess I ain't."

She snuggled into his chest, kissing his nipples. "What if I can get you goin' again?"

Her hand closed around his cock. She jerked him, hoping for results. Raider shook his head, thinking that his stiffening length had a life of its own. She tried to pull him over on top of her.

"All right," he said. "But when we're finished, you got to

answer ever' question I ask you."

She nodded. "When we're finished."

They started in. Raider suddenly found himself in something that approached competition. Helen had as much knowledge of the male body as he had of the female form. They went through the motions, taking chances, experimenting. Helen asked him to do a couple of things he had never done before. He obliged her, half for his own pleasure and half out of curiosity. Before he reached his second climax, he had added a few tricks to his repertoire of bedroom games.

He was behind her when he came. They both collapsed, writhing on the mattress. Raider got in front of her, pulling her close. He waited for her to catch her breath before he began his inquiry.

"You were talkin' about Thornton," he prompted.

She sighed. "Okay. Did I tell you I met him in Tennessee?"

"Yeah. He was dealing cards in the cat . . . in the place where you were workin'."

She cogitated for a moment and then went back to her story. "Like I said, we met in Memphis. I liked Adrian right off. He wasn't the handsomest man in the world, but he had a way of actin' like a gentleman. Said he had to leave Connecticut when his family business went bankrupt."

"What kind of business?"

"Lumber, I think," she replied. "Or something like that. Anyway, he said he was tired of them and he was working his way west. Well, I had just about had it with . . . what I was doing, so I said I'd go with him."

She stopped. Raider rubbed her shoulder, urging her to go on. She started to cry a little.

"What's wrong, honey?"

"I feel rotten," she replied, sobbing.

Raider kissed her cheek. "Don't feel bad about us beddin' down."

She shook her head. "It ain't that. I just feel bad about tellin' you all this. Kinda like I'm doing Adrian wrong."

He exhaled, wondering which direction to take with her. "Look at it like this," he said finally, "you're just helpin' me to protect him. The more I know, the easier it'll be for me to make sure nothin' happens to him.''

The crying ran its course. ''Okay,'' she said. ''But if I don't feel like tellin' you somethin', I won't.''

He patted her bottom. ''That's agreeable. Now s'pose you tell me what happened after you and Adrian left Tennessee.''

''Adrian. I never really liked that name. Sounds like a woman.''

Raider nodded. ''Yeah, I reckon.''

Again she pondered her discourse before speaking.

She wasn't a bad woman, Raider thought. Just somebody who had been dealt a few lousy cards. She finally started up again in a defeated voice.

''I come from what used to be a good family, Raider. But the war ruined them. By the time I came along, my folks were sharecropping for the Yankee who bought our farm. When I met Adrian, he was so gentle. Still is. Anyway, we headed west and ended up on a riverboat. Adrian dealt poker and faro, and I ran the wheel of fortune. You a gambling man, Raider?''

''Ever'thing but faro,'' he replied. ''I can't stand faro.''

''Neither could Adrian.'' She laughed. ''I really liked running that wheel, though. I'd draw a crowd with the outfit I was wearing. It was a lot better than whoring. There, I said it.''

''Don't be hard on yourself, Helen.''

She kissed him. ''Thank you. Where was I? Oh yeah, we left the riverboat after a month. The train took us to San Antonio. Adrian worked in a bank for a while and I took in wash. God, I hated that. But we got by until Adrian ran into the men he's working for now.''

Raider sat up a little. ''You mean Thornton isn't the main boss?''

She shook her head. ''No, they're in Phoenix. Adrian is in on the deal. He has ten percent. And they're paying him a salary to stay here. He's more or less working for them.''

''Tell me who they are.''

''Two of them are brothers. Matt and David Benedict. Then there's the big man, Alexander McPeters. He's the one who put up most of the money for the land they're buying.''

Raider got up, searching in his vest pocket for a match. He

torched the oil lamp on the nightstand. Then he rummaged in his saddlebag for a stubby pencil and a brown piece of paper.

Helen leaned up on one arm, her eyes squinting from the light. "What are you doing?"

"I want to write them names down. Just in case I need them."

She dropped back on the bed. "Suit yourself."

"How do you spell them?"

She spelled out all three names for him.

Raider put the paper back in his saddlebag. When he turned toward the bed again, he stopped. Helen glanced up at him, perplexed at the wide-eyed expression on the big man's face.

"What's wrong?" she asked.

He shrugged. "You just look so damned beautiful layin' there like that."

She put her hands behind her head. "Yeah?" Her breasts jiggled a little. "Maybe you'd like to get back in here with me and do somethin' about it."

"Maybe." He folded his arms. "But I got a few more questions I want to ask you."

She pursed her lips in a mock kiss. "Fire away."

"Where'd Thornton meet these men?"

"At the bank," she replied. "They were friends with his boss. When the boss spoke highly of Adrian, they asked him to come west to run Adobe Sands. Hell, I thought we were coming to some town that would be nice. Adrian thought so too. You should have seen the look on his face when we rode into town. For a minute I thought he was going to back out of the deal. But I reckon they're paying him enough to keep him here." She chortled. "I tell you, if I got the chance to clear out, I'd go in a minute."

He squinted at her. "You stay here of your own free will, don't you?"

She laughed. "Yes, I do. I guess it's better to be a bored queen than a whore who's excited."

She patted the bed, inviting him to come back.

He shook his head. "Who hired Clanton?"

"I'm not sure. He just showed up one day. I don't think Adrian sent for him, but he was glad to have some protection.

The padre was starting to go crazy by then.''

"You ever meet the padre?" he asked.

"Sure. He's Spanish. Handsome as the devil himself." She sighed. "You know, I never figured him for the violent kind. He seemed so gentle. Then he started to get huffy about Adrian buying out the homesteaders."

Raider eased over toward her, sitting on the edge of the bed, staring into her brown eyes. "Tell me true, Helen. Has Thornton been hard-assin' any of these settlers, tryin' to get them to leave by threatenin' 'em?"

"No."

"You sure?"

She touched his hand. "Adrian never leaves the hotel for more than a few minutes at a time. Then he only goes to the bar to collect any money, and there ain't never much of that."

Raider grimaced. "What about Clanton? He ever done any rough stuff that you know about?"

She shook her head. "I don't know of any. I heard him and Adrian arguing one day. Clanton wanted to use guns to make the deal come along a little faster, but Adrian warned him not to. And when most of them sodbusters showed up to get their money, they were thanking Adrian like he was some long-lost uncle."

"Nobody caused trouble?"

"Not really." Her brow wrinkled. "A few of them said nasty things to Adrian. Accused him of picking their bones. But he pointed out that he hadn't been the one to make their farms and ranches fail."

"What about the Calders? The ones out by the Little Sands River."

Helen smiled. "Just plain hardheaded. Had them a few cows out there, but they never made them into a herd. I met the girl once. Carrie Calder. She's pretty in a plain sort of way. Works like a dog; her daddy does too. She had a couple of brothers, but some say they went back east. Got tired of Arizona. Let me tell you, this place is easy to get tired of."

Raider stood up, pacing back and forth.

"What's wrong?" Helen asked.

"I can't put it to rest," he replied. "If things are going the way you say, then that padre doesn't have any business shootin' up the place. I want to know what set him off. What made him torch his own church.''

He caught her brown eyes staring at his crotch.

"Are you finished with your questions?'' she asked.

"Almost. What do you know about the bartender and the liveryman?''

"Just that both of them are planning to leave as soon as they've saved enough money. Adrian is paying them well, but neither one of them wants to stay.''

"Makes sense,'' Raider replied. "What's that old sayin' about rats and a sinkin' ship?''

Helen smiled at him. "They leave as soon as the water hits their noses. Come on, get back here in this bed. I'm ready again. How about you?''

He stretched out beside her. When she started to grab his cock, he gripped her wrist, stopping her. "One more thing. If you hear anything that might help my investigation, you come tell me. Okay?''

"You put that thing inside me and I'll do anything you say.''

He let go of her wrist. Her hand gripped his cock, pulling him from half-erect to full-length. When he was hard, they renewed their contest, trying to find something that neither one of them had tried.

Raider climaxed for the third time, a number that was dwarfed in comparison to Helen's releases.

He began to lose interest as his eyelids drooped. Helen tried to revive him, but to no avail. She got up, searching for her nightgown. She was dropping it back over her head when the knock on the door caused Raider to spring up out of the bed.

"Raider?''

It was Thornton.

"Raider, have you seen Helen?''

The big man felt his mouth go dry. "Hell no, Thornton. She ain't in here. Why you wakin' me up?''

"Sorry,'' Thornton replied. "I thought I heard somebody out in the hall. I'll try the kitchen.''

Raider looked at the wide-eyed woman. "What now?''

She waited a moment, then opened the door and peered out.

"I can get to the kitchen through Adrian's office. There's a hallway there. When I slip out, you call him back here and stall him."

She left without looking back.

Raider went to the door and called Thornton's name. The dapper gentleman from Connecticut came through the hallway shaking his head. He wore a blue satin robe that shimmered in the light from Raider's room.

"What is it, Raider?"

The big man opened his door wide so Thornton could see inside his room. "Did you just knock at my door or was I dreamin'?"

"I woke you," Thornton replied. "I can't find Helen."

"Here I am. I was just getting a drink on this hot night." She sashayed down the hall with a glass of milk in her hand.

Raider closed the door to hide his nakedness. He listened as Thornton told her that he had just looked in the kitchen. Helen replied that she had been in the back, using a piss-pot. Thornton told her that he had heard footsteps that had awakened him.

"Of course, I was going to the kitchen, Adrian. Come on, let's go back to bed."

They tromped off down the hall, fussing as they went.

Raider breathed easier. Thornton had bought it. The big man turned out the lamp and reclined on the bed again.

He tried to think about everything Helen had told him, but his head would not cooperate. So he leaned back on the pillow, closing his eyes. He drifted off in a hurry, sleeping peacefully until morning, when he was awakened by the loud crowing of a rooster outside his window.

CHAPTER TEN

Raider saddled up and left Adobe Sands without a word to anyone, including the sleepy-eyed liveryman. The black was rested, ready to be given his head to run. Raider held him still behind the general store for a few minutes, searching for tracks from the gunslinging padre. The ground was too hard to render hoofprints, so he turned the stallion due west and galloped for the vague impression of the hills against the morning sky.

The air was fresh and cool, in no way signaling the demon of a killer sun that baked the arid plain from late morning until dusk. Looking around him, Raider wondered what possessed a man to put down roots where only sage and greasewood would grow. Even at fifteen cents an acre the land was hardly a good deal. He had to keep the stallion at a slower pace to avoid rocks and prairie dog holes.

An hour into his ride, Raider came up on a slight rise that overlooked a shallow basin. A river ran through the middle of the basin—the Little Sands, from what he had been told. He also spied the wisp of smoke from the small house that rested by the riverbank. The Calders' place. And they were home.

The black walked down into the basin. Raider turned him along the river. Judging by the cattle skulls on the riverbank, the Little Sands was a seasonal tributary, fed by the summer rains and the spring thaw. The water bubbled along the rocky bed, but it wouldn't be long before it dried up and left behind dry stones as smooth and polished as the bleached cow heads.

He crossed the Little Sands, which barely drew a foot on

the black's forelegs. As he came closer to the house, he reined back, studying the square structure. It was a rock house, constructed from river stones that had been mortared with natural clay. The smoke had stopped in the chimney.

Raider shook the black's reins, approaching the house with clear-eyed caution. His hand hung loosely over the Peacemaker, close enough for a fast draw but far enough to let the sodbusters know that he didn't plan to use his pistol. If Thornton had been telling the truth—that he had dealt peaceably with the homesteaders—then there wouldn't be a problem.

"That's as far as you ride, mister!"

The voice had come from an older man. He had eased around the side of the rock house with a rusty scattergun pointed in Raider's direction. The big man halted the black.

"Now just turn around and go back to where you came from."

The second command had been delivered by a woman. She stood at the other corner of the house holding a Winchester. She waved with the barrel, indicating the direction that Raider should take.

He tipped back his Stetson and held out his hands in a nonthreatening gesture. "No need for them shootin' irons," he replied. "I come to see the Calders. If you be them."

The woman and the old man looked at each other for a long moment.

Finally the woman answered in a plucky voice, "Ain't no need for you to come any closer. Just speak what you come to say and then leave us be."

"I'm a Pinkerton agent," he called. "I come in search of the truth."

"Ha!" the woman replied. "Thornton sent you to threaten us. To tell us you'll burn us out if we don't sell to him."

Raider shook his head. "Thornton hired me, but I ain't necessarily on his side. He says he's been treatin' you sodbusters—"

"We ain't sodbusters, we're homesteaders!" the woman cried.

"All right, homesteaders, then." He kept his hands out away

from his sides. "Thornton says he's been fair with everyone. That's what I come out here to find. I'm lookin' for Carrie Calder."

Again the man and woman regarded each other.

It was the girl that spoke. "Put your guns on the ground and come on in."

Raider nudged the black with his legs. The stallion started forward. He raised his hands over his head.

"I said put down your guns!"

Raider shrugged. "I'm bettin' you ain't gonna shoot me."

The black kept coming.

"Why you think that?" the old man asked.

He was close enough to see their faces. "Because you seem like honest, God-fearin' people. And I ain't here to do you no wrong."

The girl came out to grab the reins of the black. When she looked up, Helen Mallory's description came to mind: "pretty in a plain sort of way." She was younger than Raider had figured. Her eyes were clear, and she had the fragile look of a girl who might be ultimately defeated by the rigors of the homesteader's life.

"I'm gonna get down," Raider said. "If you shoot me, you ain't gonna have nobody on your side."

"Drop them guns!" Carrie Calder insisted.

The old man moved toward Raider. "Carrie, leave him be."

"Pa, he . . ."

The old man extended his hand. "Name's Sherman Calder. And you?"

"Raider." The big man dropped out of the saddle and shook the old man's hand. "I meant it when I said I'm here to find out the truth."

Sherman Calder spat a wad of tobacco into the dust. "Well, Raider, best come on in and sit down. You had breakfast yet?"

Raider shrugged. "No, I reckon I ain't."

The girl pushed past him, leading the black toward a hitching post. "Pa, we ain't got enough to feed ourselves, much less a big goon like him."

"Hush up, Carrie!" the old man snapped. "He's a guest of

our'n, and we're gonna treat him as such.''

She tied up the stallion, cast a pouty glance at Raider, and hurried into the stone house.

Raider nodded at the rocky structure. "Fine job. You lay the stone?"

"Yes, sir," replied Sherman Calder. "Pulled 'em out of the riverbed myself. Dug the clay in the hills. Took me nigh on to a year to get it up, but I finally done it. Had my boys to help me back then."

"Some say they lit out and left you," Raider offered.

Calder squinted at the big man. "You did say you's here to find out the truth, didn't you?"

"I did."

"Come on inside, mister. I'll tell you all the truth you want to hear."

The interior of the stone house was bigger than most cabins or sod huts but not by much. Raider wondered how the homesteaders did it, living four to a one-room place. It took a lot of guts to homestead.

Carrie Calder stood at the stove, ladling hotcakes into a big skillet. She shot contemptuous looks at Raider, still unable to believe in his good intentions. She slammed a plate in front of him and offered dark molasses to sweeten the cakes.

"Takin' the food out of our mouths!" she muttered.

Raider ate quickly, wolfing down the hotcakes. Sherman offered him a steaming cup of coffee. He apologized for the fact that they did not have any sugar for sweetening. Raider replied that molasses would be fine.

The old man lowered his head, looking defeated. Raider wondered how long it would be before he started to talk. But when he finally did open his mouth, the big man heard a story that was worth waiting for.

Sherman Calder's sorrowful voice was slow and steady. He'd pause once in a while, rub his head, and stare into his coffee cup. Then he'd raise up with a new energy inside him—the energy of a man who was not yet ready to give up on life.

"Let me see, Mr. Raider, I told you about my neighbors. All good men. Me and the others all got here close within the same year. Billy Jacobs, Horst some-Swedish-name-I-can't pronounce. Harold Youngblood, Jimmy Witt, Andy Green. Andy was the one you saw in town.''

Raider eyed the old man. ''You heard about that? All the way out here?''

Sherman nodded. ''I heard. Andy came out to tell me. He warned me to leave, but I just can't.'' A kind nod from the old gentleman. ''Andy said you helped him get his horses back.''

''I did,'' Raider replied. ''But Thornton assured me that was the only time things got rough.''

Carrie leaned in to fill their coffee cups. ''Ha!'' she scoffed. ''Thornton burned out two families before he persuaded everyone else to sell. Jimmy Witt and the Youngbloods had to leave without a thing. They didn't even have the money from selling out to Thornton.''

Raider lifted the steaming cup. ''What about the others?''

''Sold out,'' Sherman replied. ''Jacobs and the Swede got twenty cents an acre. They both lit out for California.''

Raider leaned forward. ''Tell me about the raids.''

''I did.''

''No, I mean the particulars.''

The old man sighed. ''Well, both raids come right at dusk. Masked men, as far as we know. Hit hard and rode out. Left the place burnin'. First raid got Jacobs. My boys and the others laid for them the second time. Got a couple, but my sons were both . . .'' He hung his head.

Carrie put her hands on her father's shoulders. ''He can't believe they're gone. I can't either.''

''Were they killed by the padre?'' Raider asked.

Sherman looked up. ''No. They were killed by Clanton and his men.''

''You're sure it was Clanton?''

''Who else?'' replied the girl. ''He came to talk to us a few days ago. Said Thornton would buy us out fair and square. Said we'd regret it if we didn't sell.''

''Another raid,'' Sherman said softly. ''It won't be hard to root us out. Not against all those guns. I know Clanton's got a dozen men in town.''

Raider nodded. "Yeah, I wondered about that. But Clanton doesn't seem to be anything more than a bodyguard for Thornton."

"He led them raids!" Carrie insisted.

The big man leaned back, folding his hands. "You saw him?"

Carrie lowered her head. "No. But he did it."

"Thornton keeps tellin' me there hasn't been any trouble," Raider offered. "He says the padre has been causin' all the grief."

Sherman Calder's old eyes flashed with angry fire. "The padre helped my boy. Tried to save his life. Brought him back here and tended him for a whole day. Till he passed on. I was glad a man of God was here, even though I never been anything more than a foot-washing Baptist from Alabama."

"What's wrong with leavin'?" Raider asked. "Just take back your money and use the profit to move on. I mean, no offense, but this land is as fallow as an old mule."

Carrie backed away from her father. "You see. I told you he was here to make us leave."

"No," Raider started, "I was just—"

"Never!" old Calder cried, raising his finger. "I'll never give in to the forces of evil. I'll fight to my death. I know this land isn't worth a plug nickel for farming, but that doesn't mean nothing. We had a man from the railroad through here, a surveyor. Said if we hung tight, the railroad might offer us a dollar an acre for this land. For all the land through here. Said all we had to do was wait."

Raider's black eyes brightened. "Now you're talkin', Mr. Calder!"

The old man gawked at him. "What?"

Raider slapped his knee. "You just gave me somethin' to work with. A reason why Thornton wants all of the homesteaders out of here as soon as possible. Now it makes sense to me that if he waited you out, it wouldn't be long before you'd have to sell anyway."

Calder nodded. "That's right. I'm down to my last dollar."

"But if these raids came like you said they did—"

"They did!" Carrie interjected.

"—then that means Thornton knows the railroad may be comin' through here any day. Not even the tracks, just the deal to secure the land. And that means he's lyin' to me. But why would he call me in? Unless he just wants me to get rid of the padre."

Father and daughter were both staring at him.

He clapped his hands. "Did you talk to the padre while he was here, Mr. Calder?"

"O' course."

"Did he own up to shootin' any of Thornton's men?"

The old man shook his head. "No. And I didn't ask him."

"But he was there, during the raid, I mean?"

Calder nodded. "Yep. How else would he have found my boy?"

Raider put it together, the way it looked best with the pieces interlocking. Thornton and Clanton were lying to him about harassing the homesteaders. Clanton led raids, wearing a mask to disguise himself. And the padre had fought with the sodbusters against the raiding parties. But why the hell would Thornton call him in if he knew Raider would find out the truth?

"Mr. Raider?"

He looked up into Carrie's round eyes.

"Would you like some more coffee?" she asked.

Raider held out his cup. "This thing gets more confusin' ever' minute."

"What's botherin' you?" the girl asked.

"Thornton," Raider replied. "He don't seem like the type to hurt people, even if he knew the railroad was comin'. The way he denies that he's done anythin' to hurt you folks. I can usually tell when a man's hidin' somethin', but dog me if that man don't have me fooled. And Helen . . ." He stopped himself. "Well, never mind."

Carrie blushed and turned away from the table.

Sherman Calder laughed a little. "High-strung girl."

"So is Helen."

Raider drained the cup of coffee and reached into his vest pocket. "Mr. Calder, I figure I done et you out of house and home with that breakfast. Here, I want you to take this."

He slapped a double eagle on the table.

The old man's eyes widened. "That's twenty dollars."

"If you need any more than that, you just whistle," Raider replied.

Sherman shook his head proudly. "Can't cotton to no charity. You just put that double eagle back in your pocket."

"Pa!" Carrie moved forward a little. "Pa, if he's offering—"

"I won't take it!" her father insisted.

Carrie leaned down. "It could be a loan. We can pay him back when the railroad buys our land." She looked up at the big man. "Would that be agreeable to you, Mr. Raider? I mean, we have more than a hundred acres here. At a dollar an acre, we would have enough—"

Raider held up his hand. "Save it. You earned that money when you told me the truth about the raids on the sodbusters. I reckon Thornton figured I wouldn't believe you. But I reckon I do."

"We can show you proof," Carrie replied emphatically.

Raider pointed at the gold piece. "Then you're still workin' for me. And I'll get the money from the home office. Tell 'em I had to hire some operatives."

Carrie reached over to pick up the coin. "Mister, you got yourself an operative, as long as it ain't nothin' sinful."

"Somebody's got to take me to one of the spots where one of your neighbors was burned out."

The old man grunted. "Can't ride that dad-blamed mule."

Carrie reached for a floppy felt hat on a wall peg. "I can. I'll take him straight down to where the Youngbloods used to live."

She hurried out the door. Clad in her faded jeans and green coat, the girl looked more like a drifter than a woman. The big man had to admit that he appreciated her spunk. He stood up from the table.

"Be careful," Sherman Calder warned. "You done stepped right into the middle of it."

"I reckon I have, old-timer. I reckon I have."

The whole thing still didn't feel right to Raider. If Thornton was really behind the attacks on the homesteaders, the last person he would have wanted along was a Pinkerton. Unless he figured Raider could be bought sooner or later, like everyone else.

"Keep that scattergun close by, Mr. Calder."

The old man spat tobacco in a can on the floor. "By golly, I know how to use it, too!"

Raider went outside and untied the black. The girl came around the house on the back of a broken-down mule. Raider started to ask her where she found food for the animal, but he decided he didn't care.

He swung into the saddle of the stallion. "We could ride double," he offered. "Save us a lot of time."

She urged the mule forward. "No, that wouldn't be proper."

Raider fell in beside her, easing the black next to the mule.

She would not look at him, but finally said, "I appreciate what you did for me and my pa. That money'll help us hold out awhile. We ain't crazy, you know. We just bought land in the wrong place."

Looking over the bare plain, Raider tended to agree with her.

They entered a hilly area at the base of what now appeared to be full-fledged mountains. Raider did not recognize the particular range, and he was sure he had never been there before. He guided the black until Carrie Calder reined back on the mule. They balanced on a hilltop that looked down on the remains of a former settlement.

The house had been burned to the stone foundation.

"Mr. Youngblood brought that lumber all the way from Adobe Sands. Said he got a fair price for it for a place with no railroad. It only took about an hour for it to burn down." She seemed to be out of tears. Her face slacked into a despairing frown. "Stone don't burn, Mr. Raider. Will they use dynamite to get us out?"

Raider touched his Colt. "Ain't nobody gonna make you leave, Carrie. I'll see to that." He drew the gun and spun the cylinder, making sure all six shots were in place.

"Are you really a good man?" she asked.

"Better'n some. Worse'n most." He reined the black toward the path down to the burnt ruins. "Let's have us a look."

As they descended, Raider thought he caught the glinting

flash of something in the slopes behind the abandoned homestead. A bird? He kept his eyes upward, but he did not see it again.

The homestead had been burned to the ground all right. Charred planks had already crumbled to ash in the elements. Raider stepped off the stallion, scanning the ground outside the house.

It wasn't long before he found something. "Well, well. Ain't this a sight." He picked it up and showed it to Carrie.

She studied the feathered figure. "What is it?"

"Mescalero." His fingers closed around the charm. "Maybe."

Carrie looked up from the back of the mule, peering toward the slopes overhead, gazing straight over his shoulder.

Raider looked in the same direction. "What'd you see, girl?"

"Something white," she replied. "It was moving."

"Like a hawk?"

She nodded. "I reckon."

Raider looked back down at the ground. He found cartridges from rifles and pistol shells. "This where your brothers fought, Carrie?"

"Yes."

Something clicked in Raider's head. The padre had not killed Thornton's men at all. The sodbusters had stood up for themselves. But why did Thornton want to lie about the padre and have Raider go after him?

"There, Mr. Raider. I saw it!"

He spun around to see something fluttering behind a rock. It could have been a hawk, or a mountain goat. Again he studied the slopes, but the shape was gone.

"I know I saw it," Carrie insisted.

"Keep watchin'," the big man replied. "I'm gonna sift through these ashes."

He found a stick and began to poke through the remains left by the fire. Nothing. A few pieces of pottery that hadn't melted all the way. The flames had been quick. Probably used oil-soaked torches on the roof, maybe a pail full of oil through the window.

"There," the girl cried. "It's no—"

A hawk sailed off a high rock. Raider watched as it circled in the wind current, swooping over the plain. He was about to turn back when he noticed the irregular shape against the sky.

"Do you see him, Carrie? High up?"

"Yes, I—"

"Don't scream, girl. Just act like you don't see him."

She stared into the mountains. "But it's like he wants us to see him."

Standing high on a rock, his hands on his hips, was the figure of a man. He seemed to be wearing some sort of robe, the cassock of a priest. The hood of the garment had been pulled up, leaving a point above his head.

Raider grabbed the reins of the black. "Carrie, head back to your daddy. Y'all stay put till I get there."

He swung into the saddle.

Carrie looked scared. "Are you going after him?"

"Looks like it." He turned the stallion toward the slopes. "If I ain't back by dark, go to the nearest telegraph and send a message to the Pinkerton National Agency, Fifth Avenue, Chicago. Tell 'em I'm in a heap of trouble and send somebody to help me."

"The padre won't hurt you, Raider. He's—"

"Just go! You don't want to leave your pa all by his lonesome."

"Pa!"

She shook the mule's reins, heading home.

Raider spurred the black, riding as far as he could until the mountains made passage on horseback impossible.

He dismounted, climbing in the rocks, heading for the shaded figure that stood boldy, arrogantly against the sky.

The flash was coming from the gold crucifix on his chest. Raider was close enough to see it. He kept climbing toward the man in the cassock.

The rocks ended at a path that rose gradually toward the peaks. Raider found the way slippery, scuffling for purchase with his leather-soled boots. When he was close enough to make out the rope around the padre's waist, he drew his gun and aimed it upward.

"Come on down, padre." The command echoed through

the slopes. "I mean it. If you come peaceable, there won't be any problem."

With a surprising quickness and agility, the man dropped from the rock, falling out of sight.

Raider could not believe his eyes. "Son of a bitch."

He holstered the Colt and started climbing. He struggled to the spot where the man had been standing. He looked all around. Where was the padre now?

Loud laughter echoed from behind him.

Raider wheeled around to see the man standing on another rock some two or three hundred feet up the mountain.

The big man found the path and started skyward again. Sweat broke over his forehead as the sun climbed along with him. Once more he got close enough to see the padre's faded brown robe. The crucifix mirrored the sun's golden rays.

Raider drew the Peacemaker. "Padre! I'm tired of playin' games. Are you comin' with me, or do I have to—"

The big man yelled with pain.

He looked down to see the slender arrow sticking out of his leg. It wasn't long, more like a dart. The head had pricked his calf, lodging just under the skin.

Raider pulled out the arrow, lifting it from his leg. "Mescalero," he muttered.

They had poisoned him. He felt his head starting to spin. His stomach flip-flopped, trying to get out of his body.

"Mescalero."

The arrow fell from his fingers. He slipped on the rocks, thudding against a boulder. His arms closed around the rock, and he hung on until he lost consciousness.

CHAPTER ELEVEN

There were voices around him. He heard the men talking in Spanish, arguing in a place where the words seemed to echo in darkness. Raider tried to open his eyes, but like a man caught in a waking nightmare, he could not. The voices went on a little longer, and then he felt the coolness of a moist cloth on his face.

He tried to move, but his arms and legs were frozen. What the hell had happened to him? He had been in bed with Helen . . . no, other events had transpired since then. He remembered riding with a girl—Carrie Calder. They had gone to the burnt-down house. Then he was in the mountains chasing someone. The priest! And the pain in his leg!

He groaned and tried to sit up. A hand pushed him back down. He struggled, but the hand was stronger.

"You are weak, señor." The cool cloth followed the voice. "You must lie still until you regain your strength."

Raider finally managed to open his eyes. He peered through narrow slits, gazing into a light that was as fuzzy as his head. The dark face hovered over him—a face encircled by the cowl of a cassock.

Raider tried to speak, but his mouth was dry. He smacked his lips, which also felt hot and cracked. The cowled man put a clay jug to his mouth, giving him a short drink. Raider could not remember when water had tasted so good. When the man tried to take the jug away, Raider managed to grab his wrist and prolong the drink.

"Careful," the man said, his accent thick with a Spanish inflection. "You shouldn't drink too much. Not yet."

Raider leaned back against something soft. His eyes began to focus. He could see from the rocks overhead that he was in a cave. Torches and candles burned all around him. From the rustling movements to his left, he knew that there were more people in the cave with him and the man in the brown robe.

He glared at the kind, unshaven face of the priest who tended him. "You are Father Pedroza," he said softly.

The man nodded. "Sí. I am he. And you are the man brought in by Thorton. He hired you to capture me."

A weak smile broke across Raider's parched lips. "Looks like you done all the catchin', padre."

"No, señor," Father Pedroza replied, "I did not bring you here. But since you came, I am going to do my best to save you."

"You did bring me here!" He heard himself saying it, like he was listening to another person. "I saw you on the mountain. You led me into the rocks." The padre shook his head.

"No, señor. It was not I."

Raider sighed, feeling like he had been sick for a week. "Then who?"

Laughter reverberated through the rocky confines of the cave. "It was me, señor. Me and Pulido."

Raider managed to lift his head, peering to his left. He saw a brown-faced, Spanish man swigging whiskey from a tin cup. The man had a weird expression on his face, like a rummy who had been too long in the bottle. As he laughed, spittle gathered on the corners of his mouth.

"Pay no attention to him," the padre offered. "He is my worthless brother, Diego. While I worship the Blessed Virgin, he worships tequila. He also takes the herbs given to him by the Mescaleros. Tell me, señor, how any one man can shame himself this way before God?"

Raider asked for more water. After the second drink, he began to feel better. He insisted on raising up. The padre helped him until he was leaning back against the cave wall. When he was sitting, he reached to his side for his Colt, but naturally it was gone. Nobody left you a gun when they took you prisoner.

He peered over the padre's shoulder, toward a skinny, shirtless man with a bandanna tied around his head. The gray-haired man worked at a wooden bowl, grinding something with a rock. Raider could hear the stone tapping against the bowl.

Raider looked at Father Pedroza. "Who the hell is he?"

The father sighed disgustedly. "His name is Pulido. He is Mescalero, but he is so foul that even the other Apaches will have nothing to do with him. He is the one who found you. He wanted to kill you, but I would not let him."

Pulido stood up, raising his arms, coming toward Raider with his skinny body bathed in the torchlight. "I am the Keeper of the Fangs and Talons, señor." He grinned demonically. "Watch me. I will do magic."

The padre tried to shoo him away, but the skinny Mescalero reached for a twig basket on the floor of the cave. As he picked up the basket, a steady buzzing emanated from inside. Pulido reached in and took out the biggest rattlesnake Raider had ever seen.

"He is my god," said the Keeper of the Fangs and Talons. "Not like the God of the padre. My god is here, where I can see and feel him. Would you like to feel him, señor?"

Raider snarled at the skinny man, "Git that damned thing the hell away from me, boy, before I . . ." His head began to spin. He leaned back, wondering if he would ever feel strong again.

Pulido laughed. "What will you do, white man? Shoot me? But you do not have gun. No, you do not. Ha. What is the white man without his gun?"

He wrapped the snake around his shoulder, keeping a careful grip on the reptile's head. The damned thing must have been fifteen feet long and as big around as a telegraph pole. Raider rested his head against the rock.

The padre dabbed his face with the wet cloth. "He is mad, señor. All of his kind are mad. They do not rely on God, but on the alchemist's potions. They are savages, pagans. Never trust them."

Raider grabbed the priest's wrist. "What's goin' on, padre? Why didn't you just go ahead and kill me?"

The padre flashed a patronizing but benevolent smile. "I am a man of God, señor. I cannot kill anyone."

Raider squinted at the priest. "But Thornton said you killed five of his men. Said you gunned them down."

"He is lying," Pedroza replied. "I have not killed anyone. How could I break one of God's commandments?"

"He said you were loco," Raider continued. "Said you burned your own church to the ground."

Again laughter resounded from the other side of the cave. Diego Pedroza, the padre's drunken brother, held his sides, splitting with laughter. The Mescalero joined in the chorus, chuckling derisively.

"Shut up!" the padre cried. "Both of you!" He turned back to Raider. "They are two of a kind."

"You burn your church?" Raider asked.

Father Pedroza shook his head. "No, señor. It was Thornton's men. When I spoke out to the homesteaders, the people of Adobe Sands, they threw torches into my church. They accused me of things I did not do, and I had to take to the hills. I am forced to hide like a rat, with these two rats."

Raider studied the padre's face. What had Helen Mallory said? *As handsome as the Devil himself.* Was Pedroza flat-out lying?

"They saw you, padre," Raider insisted. "During the two raids on the sodbusters, you were seen with a gun in your hand."

"I never killed anyone!" the father cried. "Thou shalt not kill."

Raider nodded. "I heard the Good Book spouted before by men who didn't mean a word of it."

The father's face turned red. "I tell you, it was not me. I was not there during the raids."

"Sherman Calder said you tended one of his boys after he was shot by Thornton's men."

A deep sigh from the padre. "I was there after. I heard the shooting. I came down to help the homesteaders. But it was not as you think. I did not have a gun. I tried to help the son of Señor Calder. He is a good man. They were all good men until Thornton came."

"Padre, I saw you myself, last night when you took a shot at me and then again today, on the mountain."

Father Pedroza stood up, glaring at the big man. "Lies! I never shot at you. I was never on the mountain today. You are lying, señor. It is you who have come to do me harm. It is you who are working for Thornton. Clanton was not strong enough to defeat men of faith, so he brought you in to finish the job."

"I ain't Thornton's hired gun," the big man insisted. "I'm here to find out the truth. Whatever the hell that is."

A shriek rose from the drunken brother. He stood up on legs that were too wobbly from tequila. The liquid spilled from his cup as he staggered toward them. His face was contorted with drunken rage.

"Truth!" he cried. "What do you know of truth? If truth were a snake, you'd step on it and it would bite you and you'd be too stupid to die. You would not know the truth if it stared you in the face."

Father Pedroza moved toward his brother. At first Raider thought the padre was going to hit the drunken man, but he only took Diego's arm and led him back to a blanket on the cave floor. He made his brother sit down with the bottle of tequila. Diego filled his cup again, teetering on the edge of passing out.

The padre came back toward Raider, shaking his head. "I am sorry, señor. He is not the man he once was. Can you believe he was a soldier in the Mexican army? A captain no less. He had a wife and a child, but they died of cholera when we first came to Adobe Sands. He has never been the same."

Raider drew a long breath. "He ain't the first one I seen give in to liquor. If I was you, though, I'd keep him away from that Mescalero."

The padre turned back to look at Pulido, who was still fussing with the rattlesnake. "I know. It is terrible that we must seek refuge with this dog of a man. Look at him. He worships the very creature that tempted Eve and forced our first parents out of the garden. A devil, that one."

Raider tried to climb to his feet. The padre urged him to sit down, to stay still until he was truly strong enough to walk. The poison would wear off eventually. Pulido had told him that. It had been Pulido who had shot the dart into his leg. The big man felt so weak that he could do little more than obey the father's command.

His black eyes lifted to the priest's kind face. "If you ain't gonna kill me, padre, what are you gonna do?"

Pedroza nodded, a hand to his chin. "I have pondered that question since they brought you here. You say you are a good man, on the side of truth. This is what I want to believe. And I have heard that you helped a man when you first came to Adobe Sands. Is this true?"

"Yep. I helped one of them sodbusters get back his horse. I also gave the Calders some money." Raider chuckled until his laughter turned to coughing. "I reckon that makes me a good man," he said, "even though you might not say it if you knowed some of the things I done."

Pedroza knelt down, patting Raider's shoulder. "None of us is free from sin, señor. I will pray for your forgiveness."

Raider eyed him cautiouly. "You still ain't told me what you plan to do with me."

The padre met his gaze. Raider felt a jolt, the power of the man's strength and the conviction. Could a man with the fire of God in his eyes be capable of killing other men with a six-gun?

"I want your solemn word," Pedroza said, holding up the wooden cross that hung around his neck. "Tell me that no harm will come to me. That you will not hurt me once you have regained your strength."

Raider nodded.

"Touch the cross," the padre insisted.

Raider hesitated. "I don't know, padre."

"Do you believe in God?"

The big man nodded. "But I ain't sure He'll understand if I—"

"Touch the cross. Then I will have your word."

Raider touched the cross. "You got my word."

The padre nodded. "Thank you. I must leave for a while. Some of the homesteaders come at night, to receive communion and let me hear their confessions. I must hurry or they will become scared and go home."

Raider glanced over the padre's shoulder. "You gonna leave me alone with them two?"

Pedroza nodded. "But I will also leave you this."

He took Raider's Colt .45 from beneath his cassock. He put it in Raider's hand. It was so heavy that the big man almost could not lift it in his weakened state.

The padre's eyes were wide. "You could kill me now, señor. You could shoot all three of us and crawl out of here."

When Raider thumbed back the hammer, the padre jumped away.

Raider smiled weakly. "Just seein' if it works, padre. Looks like you left the bullets in there."

Pedroza shook his head. "I wish that I could trust in men the way that I trust in God. I must go." He started to turn away.

"Padre?"

He looked at Raider over his shoulder. "Yes?"

"When you come back, I want you to help me find out the truth. I got to know what's going on. I'm paid to do that, not to hurt people. If you didn't try to kill me or Thornton's men, somebody did. And they got a reason for it. Comprende?"

The padre smiled. "The Lord will reveal His truth sooner or later."

"One more thing." He raised the barrel of the Peacemaker. "Either one of them boys tries anything funny, I'll plug 'em before you can say a short prayer. Got it?"

Pedroza gestured toward the snoring figure of his brother. "Diego will not do you harm." He glared at the Mescalero. "I do not care about this one. If you must shoot him, it will not matter."

Pulido looked up from the snake basket. His eyes glowed like shiny gold in the torches and candles. He laughed, a hollow sound that chilled Raider to the bones. The big man held the Colt close to his chest, praying that he could keep his eyes open and not fall asleep.

Raider saw himself stumbling in the sand. The sun seared his bare back, and the hot ground scorched his feet. His erratic steps took him toward a pool of purple water that glistened with cool ripples. Dry mouth and red throat, the taste of thirst like a fever in his body.

He dived into the water, which immediately turned to sand. When he came up, his head was covered with scorpions and he heard the rattling of a desert snake in his ear. He opened his mouth to scream but there was no voice left in him.

Raider opened his eyes. He raised up, drawing a gasping breath. His pupils focused on the reptilian shape before him. The Mescalero's rattler was looking him straight in the face. The buzzing in his dream had been real. He had fallen asleep in spite of his efforts to stay awake.

He brought up the Colt. "Back off me, Injun."

Pulido, the self-proclaimed Keeper of the Fangs and Talons, jumped back, taking the rattler with him. "No! Do not shoot. Do not kill him."

Raider tried to stand up, but he was still weak from the potion that had been inflicted on him. His mouth was as dry as a bale of Alabama cotton. He glanced toward the priest's brother, Diego, who was fast asleep on the thick blanket.

Pulido moved toward the big man again.

Raider lifted the Colt. "Stay back."

The Mescalero eased away, dropping the rattler in the twig basket. He stood still, peering at Raider. The big man licked his lips, wishing he had a gallon of spring water.

Pulido grinned maniacally. "You are thirsty. I will get you water. I will find you something to drink."

Raider did not trust the Mescalero as he receded into the shadows of the cave. He rummaged around for a few minutes, then came back into the torchlight carrying a clay gourd. He lifted the vessel toward Raider. "Here, white man. Drink."

Raider did not want to take the liquid. He looked at the sleeping drunkard. "Diego!" No response. "Diego!"

Pulido pushed the gourd in Raider's face. "Drink or you will die."

A fire had started in his gullet. Raider nodded. The Mescalero put the gourd to his lips. Raider drank for a long time, the liquid cold and bitter. When he broke off, the Keeper of the Fangs and Talons backed away, smiling.

The big man realized he had made a mistake.

Pulido grinned, his voice coming out of his mouth like the hissing of the giant rattlesnake. "Now you will see," he whispered. "You will know the secrets of El Dorado."

Raider did not really hear him. His head began to turn like a carousel, first slowly and then more and more quickly. He put the Colt on his lap, wondering if he had the strength to fire it.

"What'd you put in that drink?" he moaned. "Tell me!"

The Mescalero ignored him. He moved into the shadows, emerging again with a yellow, circular object in his grasp. He pushed the object close enough for Raider to see. It was a golden plate with ceremonial markings etched in the gold surface.

Raider could not protest. Pulido's potion had taken over his senses. It felt like the dream, only now his eyes were open, and he was suddenly aware of the Apache's lethal tone.

"Long ago," the shaman started, "to the south and east, a man dressed in gold. He lifted his eyes and arms to the sun, to pray to the great god in the sky. 'Go to the north,' the god told him. And the man walked until he saw the great river."

Raider was acutely aware of each word. His stomach turned over and over. He felt like vomiting, but he did not have the strength to move. He saw the Mescalero before him, clad in gold like the man in the story.

"El Dorado," the Indian rasped. "The golden man. He crossed the great river and walked toward the setting sun. He touched the mountains and turned them to gold. His breath turned the ground to gold. He built the great city that wore his name—El Dorado."

Raider gritted his teeth. "Shut up! Shut your goddamned mouth!"

Pulido laughed, his face taking the shape of the rattlesnake's head. "The white men came. They looked for the city of gold, but they could not find it." He held up the plate. "I have the way. I know where to find the city of gold. It is here." He indicated the markings on the gold.

It was the drink, Raider thought. The Mescalero's loco-juice had hold of his head, making him see things. He strained to focus through the haze. Pulido's head came into view but then vanished again. The big man saw a wolf standing in front of him.

"Get away from me!" he cried.

Pulido's hand pointed straight out. "To the west, in the

desert. The city of gold is there. It is hidden, but you can find it. I will take you. You will find it.''

Raider closed his eyes. A myriad of shapes and colors swirled in the darkness. He lost his sense of equilibrium. A sensation of falling gripped him. He opened his eyes to see the snake again.

"El Dorado!" the shaman cried.

A city of gold. Something popped inside him. He wanted the gold. He needed it to free him from Allan Pinkerton and Titus Tilden. How he hated them and all their kind. Sitting back on their butts while he went out to do their dirty work. Gold would free him. He shook his head. It was the drink. The damned drink!

Pulido kept the plate in front of his eyes. The way to El Dorado! The map, etched in the same gold that built the city. Walls and streets and buildings of the precious yellow metal.

Raider shook his head. "It can't be," he muttered. "Ain't no such thing. Get away from me."

The Mescalero put his hand on the smooth surface of the plate. Raider had never cared much for unlucky gold, but something about the plate felt right. He tried to tell himself it was the loco-juice, but the admonishing voice in his head gave way to another persuasive song—the siren's call of riches.

Pulido held up the gourd. "Drink again. You must. Go on. Drink, and you will see the city of gold."

Raider tried to get away from the mouth of the gourd. The deep, dark circle seemed to open up, beckoning him to slake his dusty throat. Liquid spilled toward him, promising to extinguish the fire on his lips.

He jerked his head to the side, spitting out the bitter brew that had fallen on his tongue.

Pulido laughed, jumping to his feet. He danced in a figure-eight pattern, chanting some nonsensical song. Raider tried to focus on him, but he saw three different shapes. The big man wondered if maybe he had died in his sleep and gone straight to hell in the bargain.

"Stop it!" he cried.

His stomach emptied, forcing a stream from his mouth. Raider fell over on his side. He tried not to gag. *Peyote,* he told himself. Peyote made you real sick.

A sense of relief was within him until his head began to spin again. He struggled to sit up. The floor didn't spin as much when he was sitting up.

Pulido leaned over him, grinning that savage smile. Maybe he was the devil. Raider had tried to kill the devil once, only Lucifer hadn't been real, just a man in disguise.

Maybe the Mescalero was just a man.

"More drink!" he cried.

Raider raised his pistol. "More lead!" He thumbed back the hammer. His finger closed on the trigger. The effort reminded him of a time he had tried to lift an anvil.

The trigger gave way. *Click*. No charge of fire, no slug exploding from the bore. Pulido had unloaded his gun while he was asleep.

The Mescalero laughed. Raider shook his head, wanting to wake up in a warm bed. It had to be a bad dream.

"El Dorado!" the Mescalero cried. "We will go. Get up." He tugged at Raider's arm. "On your feet, white man!"

Raider swung the butt of the Colt, catching the side of the Mescalero's head. The Indian grunted and fell back to his seat. He rolled, holding his stomach like the wind had been knocked out of him.

All the big man had to do was get up and walk out. He rested his weight on his left hand. His arm collapsed. He decided to crawl out.

When he rolled to the side, he felt sick again. His eyes focused on an insect that crawled toward him. Suddenly the creature seemed to increase in size. Raider brought down the Peacemaker, squashing the bug-eyed monster.

He tried to pull himself along the ground. Where the hell was the entrance? And where was he if he got out?

The Mescalero stood up. His face was no longer smiling. The happy-coyote expression had turned to hatred.

"I was told not to kill you," he said to the big man. "But you have made the gods angry."

Raider reached for his side. His gunbelt was gone. No cartridges. He tried his back pocket. Nothing.

He kept telling himself to get up, to hammer that Apache

and force him to show the way back down the mountain.

Pulido moved toward the twig basket on the cave floor. "No El Dorado, white man. No gold for you."

Raider's face contorted into a vulture's expression. "I hate gold, you little polecat!"

His hand gripped the barrel of the Colt. He could use it like a tomahawk. He could kill with it like an iron club.

The Mescalero lifted the rattlesnake out of the basket. "You will know my god, white man. He will take you to the other side of the darkness."

"Kiss my ass," the big man replied.

In his condition, the snake looked three times as big. Pulido dropped it on the floor. Slowly it began to slither toward Raider.

He knew he didn't have a chance. The snake would be quicker. But he tried. He struck at the diamond-shaped head of the reptile, only to have it draw back.

Flashing of thick forked tongue in the torchlight. The slitted eyes seemed to widen. Raider saw three serpents weaving back and forth, coiling for the strike.

Pulido nudged the rattler with the end of a stick. "Kill him. Kill him." He began the Indian chant.

A bizarre thought came to Raider. He would grab the rattler when it bit him. He would squeeze the life out of it. Even if the venom killed him, he would not go alone. He would take the Mescalero god with him.

"Come on, you son of a bitch."

Pulido choked on his song. He glared down at the vicious black eyes that stared out of Raider's head. He did not want his snake to die.

But the rattler's head exploded with a fiery thunderclap. The body squirmed violently, whiplashing in death spasms. Pulido collapsed as well, falling next to his pet god.

Raider saw the shape moving in the torchlight. He could not make out the face, but the cowled garment was all too familiar. He wanted to thank the man who had saved him, but he found it much easier just to pass out.

CHAPTER TWELVE

He felt the heat, surrounding him like the fires of Hell. He knew he had died. When he opened his eyes he expected to see Satan welcoming him to the netherworld after a long, dreamless sleep. But it was only the sun, high overhead, that scorched and blinded him.

Raider sat up abruptly. His stomach churned inside. He looked around to see that he was sitting on a small patch of grass. Where the hell was he? And where the hell had he been?

He had to stand up. Slowly he rose to his feet, trying his weakened legs. Had he tried to stand up somewhere else? Why couldn't he remember? He staggered a few steps to test his strength. It felt damned good to walk. Why hadn't he been able to walk before?

His head throbbed with a dull aching, like he had been in a fight. A fight that he had lost. Raising his hand to shade his eyes, he gazed toward the blue sky, estimating the time from the sun. Close to noon. Did the time of day really matter?

A horse whinnied behind him. In a reflexive response, Raider drew his Colt and spun around, leveling the Peacemaker on the stallion. The black pulled at a tuft of green, nibbling without looking up. The saddle was intact, including the Winchester in the scabbard. Raider's Stetson hung on the butt of the rifle.

The big man felt a chill and then a fever. He started toward the black only to stumble on something. He looked down at the ground. A ceramic jug had been placed next to the spot where he had been sleeping.

Raider lifted the jug, sniffing the opening in the neck. The water smelled pure and fresh. He swallowed a mouthful, trying to remember another bitter taste that had captured him. But the water was clean. He drank for a long time, filling his belly.

A sweat broke over his body, chasing the chills and fever. He took off his hat and doused himself with the cool liquid, rubbing his face to clear his black eyes.

He had had a dream. A bad dream. But he couldn't remember why he had passed out in the first place. He finished the water and looked at the jug. Who the hell had left it for him?

Raider turned slowly, surveying the area. He stopped when he saw the ruins of the homesteaders' house. He recalled being there with Carrie Calder, the girl on the mule. But what had happened after that?

He did his best to remember, but only a few vague images would come to him. The priest was there in his memory, but he could not focus. Had he seen the priest after the attempt on his life in Adobe Sands?

The sun beat unmercifully on his bare head. He tromped across the grass to the stallion. He grabbed his hat and put it on to ward off the heat.

He needed more liquid. Something with a bite to it. Did he have any whiskey in his saddlebags? He lifted the flap and reached in.

His fingers hit something cold and scaly. Raider drew back. He pulled the saddlebags off the stallion and dropped them on the ground. An oozing red liquid flowed out onto the ground.

Raider kicked the saddlebags. The lifeless, serpentine shape fell out. He reached down to pick up the snake that had no head. It seemed to take forever to pull out the coiled reptile.

When Raider lifted the rattler, he saw that something had been tied to the snake's rattles. A golden cross! He dropped the rattler and pulled the cross away.

Like another headache, the memory came rushing back to him. The priest leading him into the mountains. The cave. The Mescalero. Father Pedroza's denial. The snake's head exploding. Pedroza had saved his life and set him free. Maybe the padre wasn't lying when he denied shooting Thornton's men.

Raider closed his eyes. He saw gold: a round, yellow plate. He heard Pulido's words—El Dorado. The Mescalero had told him he would be able to find the legendary lost city of gold.

He looked down at the golden cross. Maybe there was something more at stake besides the railroad. Maybe Thornton and his men knew something else.

Raider wanted to sort it out, but he was still muddled by the effects of the Indian's loco-juice. The only thing to do was ride back to Adobe Sands and confront Thornton head on. If Clanton or any of Thornton's men got in his path, Raider would just have to stop them the hard way. If it took gunplay to get the truth, the big man was more than ready.

He kicked the snake carcass away and then put the saddlebags behind the saddle of the black. When he swung onto the stallion, he felt dizzy again. He had to hang onto the saddle horn for a minute to steady himself.

Cursing the Mescalero under his breath, he nudged the black into a slow walk. He suddenly heard the Apache's chant in his head, followed by the nasal tone of his words: "I was told not to kill you." Who told him?

He rode out of the shallow valley back into the hills. He tried to look up, to see if he was being followed, but any motion of his head made him nauseous. He had seen monsters in that cave. He wondered if any of them would visit his nightmares.

His body continued to ache. The sweat had run dry. He felt thirsty again, the cotton-mouthed kind that would not go away.

The river, he told himself. The Little Sands had water in it. He would drink and bathe himself in the cold water. He felt the grizzle on his face. How long had it been since he'd shaved? How long, for that matter, had he been in the mountains? A day might have passed, but for all he knew he could have been lying by the burnt-down house for several days, even a week.

The stallion emerged on the highest ledge of the hills. Raider peered into the distance, looking at the tiny structure of the Calders' stone house. He recalled ordering the girl to go home and wait for him. The Calders would be able to tell him how long he had really been out.

He saw the river, too, glistening as it rippled through the desolate valley. He would cleanse himself in the Little Sands, a baptism worthy of any preacher—or priest.

Perched on the high ground, Raider realized he wanted to believe the padre was innocent of any wrongdoing. If Pedroza had been a heartless gunman, he would not have saved Raider from the Mescalero and his snake. A shudder went through him as he remembered the giant rattler crawling slowly toward him. Sometimes a rattler's bite wasn't lethal, but a snake that big would have enough venom to kill a buffalo.

Raider heard an echo that made him glance up. Had somebody fired a shot? He squinted toward the Calders' spread, watching as antlike riders descended on the stone cottage. Raider screamed, but no one heard him. The riders, ten or twelve of them, fired their pistols and rifles, puffs of smoke that were followed by the horrific echo.

The big man forgot his own aches and pains. He turned the black down the path, going as fast as the incline would allow him. What the hell good would he be able to do against all those men?

He decided not to think about it and just ride.

By the time he was on flatland, driving hard along the bank of the Little Sands River, a trail of thick smoke rose from the roof of the stone cottage. The black took his head, running faster than Raider could have hoped. When he was close enough to see the shapes of the marauders, he took his rifle out of the scabbard and began to fire wildly.

Two of the jayhawkers fell to the ground.

The others turned to see the big man riding down on them.

Raider reined back, steadying himself to take aim on another rider. He fired again, and a man fell from his horse. The remaining riders wasted no time returning his fire. Raider reined the black to his left, driving away from them in a wide circle. He hoped to draw them with him. If they would chase him into the mountains, he could hide in the rocks and pick them off one at a time.

But they did not follow. When the big man looked over his shoulder, he saw that the riders had turned back. He reined the black and peered toward the stone house. The smoke was thicker, darker.

Raider pulled his Colt. "Sons of bitches!"

He spurred the stallion in the direction of the attackers, who were heading the other way.

Why the hell would they run from him?

The answer popped into his head: their work was done.

Flames leapt from the roof of the house, the only part that wasn't made out of rocks. He rode past the bodies he had strewn with his Winchester. The fleeing riders were lumps in the distance now.

Raider jumped down next to the stone house, bringing up his Winchester. He fired until it was empty. His eyes strained to see if he had hit anyone. As the riders disappeared over the ridge, a lone figure stopped at the crest of the rise.

The big man squinted to make sure he was not seeing things. Even at the great distance the shape was unmistakable. The lone rider wore a cassock, the heavy brown garment of a priest.

Raider ran for the black, thinking he would give chase. The smoldering roof stopped him. Carrie Calder and her father were inside. If nothing else, they deserved a decent burial. Raider kicked open the door to see them lying dead on the floor. He dragged them out of the smoky cottage.

Both of them had been shot several times. Raider reached down, touching the errant lock of thin hair that fell over the girl's forehead. Pretty in a plain sort of way.

He looked around until he found a small shovel that was wedged in a pile of dirt near a hole that Sherman Calder had been digging. Had the old man known something? Had he been digging his own grave?

Raider finished the hole, filling it with the bodies of father and daughter. He thought about saying words over them, but there wasn't any kindness left inside him. He felt only hatred for the men who had killed them. He wanted to even the score.

Get back to Adobe Sands, he told himself.

As he started for the stallion, he caught the other dead bodies from the corner of his eye. He decided to look them over. Maybe he'd find something useful, a clue that might link them to Thornton.

They were dressed like Mescaleros. Wide headbands, colorful shirts, buckskin pants. But they weren't Indians. They were white men dressed like Apaches. Clanton's men?

Raider thought about the priest on the ridge, looking back at him. Was Father Pedroza somehow linked to Thornton? The big man could not believe it. Why would Pedroza save his life and then turn around to attack the Calders?

One thing was clear—Thornton wanted the land to be his. All of it. And that had meant burning out the homesteaders who would not sell willingly. He still could not figure out why Thornton would call in a Pinkerton, even to catch the padre. Was Thornton really that stupid?

Raider turned his eyes to the clear sky. Already the buzzards were circling the dead bodies, waiting for him to leave. He took the time to throw rocks over the Calders' grave mound, building a cairn that would discourage the scavengers. Raider hated to see good people get it, even though his experience told him that the good ones always got it first.

When the grave was covered, he started back toward the stallion.

The bodies of the dead ambushers lay bleeding in the sun. It wouldn't take them long to start stinking in the heat. The proper thing would be to plant them deep in the ground.

Raider swung onto the saddle of the black.

To hell with them, he thought. Let the buzzards pick their eyes out of their decaying skulls. Let the coyotes sink their teeth into the soft flesh of their bellies. That was all they deserved, to end up as something that would fall out of an animal's behind. They hadn't been much better in life. At least they'd be useful in death.

He spurred the stallion and drove hard for Adobe Sands.

When the desolate structures of Adobe Sands rose up in front of him, Raider slowed the lathered black. He came in carefully, Colt drawn, expecting a welcoming committee. But no one drew down on him as he tied the stallion behind the general store.

With the Peacemaker in front of him, Raider stepped cautiously down the alleyway. Most of the strength had returned to his legs, bolstered by anger and hatred toward his former employer. He poked his head out into the dusty street, looking in both directions. Nothing. Not even a sound. No dull hammering from the livery, no click of swinging doors from the saloon.

A light wind stirred the powdery sand on the street.

Raider gazed toward the hotel. No signs of movement., Thornton probably felt safe and comfortable in his nest.

The big man leaned back against the wall. He considered

riding to the barracks where Clanton kept his men. But what chance would he have against a half score of guns? Best to grab Thornton, head for Kingman, and ask the sheriff to mount a posse. With the posse behind him, Raider could come back and clean out Clanton and his rattlesnakes.

A few things still weren't clear in Raider's head, but he figured to make Thornton tell the truth, to come clean once and for all.

He took a deep breath and bolted out of the alley, running across the street as fast as his legs would take him.

The door to the hotel was open. The big man eased into the cool shadows of the lobby. He listened but did not hear anything beyond the creaking of the floor and walls. Using the Colt to lead the way, he started for Adrian Thornton's office. The door was not locked. Raider turned the knob and pushed in, aiming the Peacemaker at an empty desk.

"Son of a bitch," he muttered under his breath.

He tiptoed down the hallway, making for Thornton's bedroom. He listened at the threshold. He heard movement. Stepping back, he raised a booted foot and splintered the bedroom door.

A woman screamed.

Raider leveled the barrel of the Colt at Helen Mallory. "Where the hell is he?"

Her lips trembled. "Raider, I—"

"Where the hell is Thornton?"

Her nervous eyes focused on the bore of the pistol. "Why are you aiming that thing at me?" She looked up at his face. "And where the hell have you been for two days? You rode out of here without a word and then just disappeared. We thought you had been killed."

Raider lowered the weapon. "Yeah, I bet you did. Only I ain't been killed. I'm alive. And I want your boyfriend."

She frowned. "Adrian?"

"None other," he replied. "I want to ask him a few questions."

She smiled, coming toward him. "Why don't you ask me a few questions?"

She put her hand on his shoulder. Raider grabbed her wrist. Helen grimaced with pain.

"You're hurting me," she protested. "What's wrong with you?"

She peered up into hateful black eyes.

Raider let her go, pushing her back onto the bed. "Carrie Calder and her daddy are lyin' in a grave out at their place. Clanton and his men attacked them about two hours ago."

Her brow wrinkled. "What?"

"Don't act so surprised," he said, pointing a finger at her. "You know what your boyfriend is up to. Don't you?"

She put a trembling hand against her bosom. "Raider, I don't know what you're talking about. Adrian hasn't—"

He scowled at her. "Bullshit! Thornton has been behind the attacks on the sodbusters since he got here."

"No, I swear to you, he hasn't."

"I buried Carrie Calder today. I put her and her old man in the same hole in the ground. You tellin' me that Thornton didn't know about the raid? That he didn't send them jayhawkers out there?"

She came off the bed, pressing herself against him. "Adrian isn't that kind, Raider. I swear. If he had known about those attacks, I would have known too. A woman can tell things. Men talk in bed."

Raider pushed her away. "I bet they do. And now you're coverin' for him. You've been coverin' for him all along to protect your meal ticket."

"No, I swear to God!"

"Come clean, Helen. Tell the truth and I'll see to it that the law goes easy on you. You ain't got nothin' to lose. When Thornton's behind bars, you're gonna lose everything anyway."

She started to say something. Then her eyes swelled. She was gawking over his shoulder. Raider spun around and glared at Adrian Thornton.

The dapper gentleman smiled at the big man. "Raider. You're back. We missed you for the past two days. Suppose you'd be good enough to tell us where you were."

When he raised the Colt, Thornton's beady eyes bugged out.

"I been talkin' to priests and buryin' bodies," the big Pinkerton replied. "But I guess you know all about that."

Thornton backed up against the wall, his eyes crossed on the bore of the Peacemaker. "What are you talking about?"

"Your men raided the Calders' place today. Killed both of them. I know, I had to dig the grave."

"No," Thornton said. "It can't be. I never—"

Raider grabbed his shirtfront, slamming him against the colorful wallpaper. "You knew the railroad man was out there surveyin'. You hired Clanton to raise a gang of men, to run out them homesteaders."

Thornton's voice was meek, pleading. "Why would I offer them a good price and then run them out?"

"Because you know the railroad is gonna come through there. You know the deal for the land is gonna be cut a lot sooner than ever'body expects. That land is gonna be worth a dollar an acre before long. Ain't it?"

Thornton nodded. "All right, I knew the surveyor had been out there. He stayed right here at the hotel. But I never authorized any raids on the homesteaders. If they wanted to stay put, that was their business."

Raider laughed derisively. "How dumb do you think I am, Thornton? I was out there. I seen the house that was burnt to the ground. The one that was owned by the Youngblood family."

"I paid them top dollar!"

"What choice did they have?" the big man cried. "After they were burnt out, what else could they do?"

"I never ordered that!" Thornton insisted. "I told Clanton to lay off. Besides, why would I call you in if I were up to no good? Do you think I'm that stupid?"

Raider eased back, letting go of his shirtfront. "I been wonderin' about that, Thornton."

"And what did you decide?" he asked, straightening his clothes.

Raider exhaled. "The padre talked against you. You framed him to make it look like he was killin' people. But he wouldn't leave. So you called me in to find him. You didn't count on me learnin' the truth before I did."

"Ridiculous!" Thornton replied. "The padre was killing people. My men saw him with their own eyes."

"So did I."

Thornton gaped at the big man. "You mean you found him?"

"In the mountains."

Thornton smiled. "That's wonderful. Did you bring him back?"

Raider shook his head. "No. But he saved my life. And now I'm going to return the favor."

"How?"

"By takin' you to Kingman. I'm gonna turn you over to the sheriff, and then I'm comin' back here with a posse to get Clanton." He gestured with the barrel of the Colt. "Go on."

Thornton hesitated. His eyes bulged again. He was staring straight over Raider's shoulder. A shadow moved on the wall. Raider spun around to see Helen Mallory coming at him with an oil lamp. He stepped aside and she crashed into the wall.

As Helen Mallory slumped to the floor, Adrian Thornton ran into the hallway. Raider stepped over the woman's body, running after Thornton. He caught him by the back of his collar.

Raider put the tip of the Peacemaker in Thornton's ear. "I can kill you now or you can stand trial. What will it be?"

"Trial," Thornton replied in a raspy voice. "I tell you, I didn't do anything wrong."

"Save it for the gallows. There'll be a preacher there. You can tell him all about it."

He kept Thornton ahead of him, pushing the trembling land baron into the dusty street.

When they were at the midpoint of Adobe Sands's only thoroughfare, Raider heard the chortle of rifle levers. He looked up to see Winchester barrels pointed at him from the roofs of the hotel and the general store. Ace Clanton looked down the barrel of an old Sharps .50 caliber.

"Drop the iron, Pink-man," Clanton urged.

Raider held the Colt against Thornton's head. "Go on, Ace. You let me have it and I drop your boss man."

Clanton laughed. "You think I care about that little pissant? Shoot him if you want. But otherwise you're dead alongside him."

"Like the Calders?" Raider accused.

Clanton scoffed at the big man. "I don't know what the hell you're talkin' about."

"I buried them a couple of hours ago, Ace. You and your boys dressed up like Mescaleros for the raid. Somebody was wearin' a cassock, too. You know who that was, Clanton?"

The scar-faced man shook his head, smiling. "Ain't got a clue, big 'un. Now s'pose you just let go of Mr. Thornton and move away."

Raider looked up at the guns. There was no way out of it. If he started firing, they would get him. If he ran they would get him.

He let go of Thornton, who ran back into the hotel.

"Wise move," Clanton said. "Now drop that Peacemaker."

Raider considered letting Clanton have it between the eyes. One shot. Of course, he was buzzard chow the minute he let go of the first round. Still, killing Clanton would even things for the Calders.

"Don't try it, big 'un. This buffalo gun will cut you a new asshole in your chest."

One shot.

"I mean it, Raider."

As long as he was alive, he decided, he would have a chance to escape.

The Colt fell into the dust.

Clanton's men moved out to take him prisoner.

They locked him in the attic of the hotel, chaining him to a rafter with his hands bound behind him. At least the chain was long enough for him to sit down. He stared into the lengthening shadows, watching until darkness overtook the narrow, musty enclosure.

They left him alone. Why hadn't they killed him? He didn't figure they would even feed him, but later that evening, he heard someone on the narrow steps that led up to the attic. Keys rattled in the door. Someone pushed into the darkness. He knew who it was before the match was struck and put to the wick of a candle. Even after everything that had happened, he could not forget the sweet smell of that perfume.

"Hello, Helen. Come to laugh at me? Or did they send you to do their dirty work?"

She bent down next to him, brandishing the powdered line of her bosom. "I'm sorry, honey, I really am. I'd set you free, but I'm afraid of Clanton. He's gettin' awful pushy. I'm sorry I tried to hit you too. I just lost my head."

Raider sighed deeply. "They're gonna do somethin' to me. You got any idea what it might be?"

Her lips were drawn in a sad pout. "I ain't sure. They said somethin' about givin' you to the Indian."

Raider's eyes narrowed. "Pulido?"

"I don't know. I just heard it. Clanton said they can't just up and kill you. That'd bring too many people around lookin' for you."

Raider nodded. "Makes sense. Or maybe your boyfriend ain't got the guts to kill somebody once he's looked 'em in the eye."

She lowered her head. "Adrian's as scared as I am."

"I bet he is."

"Really, he—"

"I don't want to talk about it," Raider replied. "If you come to tease me, save it. I ain't ready to listen to any more lies."

She touched his face. "If I could change things, I'd get us both the hell out of here."

"Then unlock me and find me a gun."

She sighed, her chest rising and falling. "It ain't that easy. Adrian and Clanton are watching me close-like. I had to sneak around just to bring you some food."

She lifted some meat toward his mouth. When Raider caught the smell of warm roast, he took big bites, gulping down the beef. She had brought bread and potatoes as well. She fed him like a baby until all the food was gone.

She brushed hair away from his forehead. "You look like hell. Like you been sick."

He laughed. "Yeah, I reckon."

She hesitated, looking into his eyes.

"You fed me," he said. "You can go."

She lowered her mouth to his lips and began hungrily to kiss him. Raider could not resist her probing tongue. He kissed her back.

Helen broke away, looking into his eyes. "I thought you might like to . . . you know, do it one more time before . . ."

"Before they kill me."

She touched his crotch. "You're hard. I reckon you ain't as sick as you look. Want me to take it out?"

He considered it. Maybe it would be his last time. He felt the surge of energy in his body, the lightning bolt that accompanied arousal by a member of the opposite sex.

"Take it out," he said.

She fumbled with the buttons of his denim pants until his cock was free. Her lips closed around the head of his prick. She went down, mouthing him, using her hand, bringing him to a full erection.

"Your tits," Raider said.

She pulled down her dress, freeing her soft globes of flesh. Embracing him, she put her breasts in his face, feeling his tongue and lips on her nipples. Raider wished his hands had not been tied behind him.

He looked up at her. "How we gonna work this?"

She laid back on the floor of the attic, lifting her dress. Raider saw her thick bush of hair in the candlelight. No underpants. She had come prepared.

Raider struggled to get into position. As he got up on his knees, he lost his balance, falling straight between her thighs. When he felt her sweetness against his face, he decided to treat her the same way she was treating him. He began to lick her up and down, driving her into a frenzy.

"You're the best," she moaned, biting her finger. "The best."

He stayed at it for a few minutes until he could no longer control himself. He crawled on top of her, jabbing desperately at her crotch. When he did not find his mark, she used her hand to guide him inside.

It was awkward with his hands chained behind him, but they worked together to achieve the desired release.

When Raider rolled off her, Helen helped him back into a sitting position. She tucked his prick inside his pants and buttoned him up. When she put her palm against his cheek, Raider shrugged away.

"What's the matter?" she asked.

He scowled at her. "I took what you offered because it might be the last time I ever know a woman. But I don't have to like you, honey. I don't have to smile. You're with them that's set on killin' me. So just clear the hell out of here and let me be.''

"Raider, I'm sorry, I truly am.''

"Just go. Before they find you here.''

She picked up the plate and the candle. "I'll try to get you out of here," she insisted. "I'll do my best to—''

The door swung open. Ace Clanton stood in the threshold. His eyes glared in the candlelight. He stomped in, coming face to face with the woman.

"What the hell are you doin' here?'' he cried.

"I just thought he ought to have some supper—''

Raider flinched when Clanton slapped her. "Why don't you pick on somebody your own size, Ace?''

Clanton pointed toward the door. "Get out of here, you whore. Now!''

Helen ran out, holding her cheek. She did not look back at Raider. The big man couldn't say he blamed her. He knew there was no way for her to get him out now. Clanton had big plans.

"You're goin' on a little trip, Pinkerton. You ready to ride?''

Raider did not reply.

Clanton took a bandanna out of his pocket. He wrapped the cloth around Raider's head, blindfolding him. The big man hoped his hands would be untied, but Clanton only unlocked the manacle that fixed the chain to the attic rafter. He lifted Raider to his feet and started pushing him toward the door.

"Gonna give me to the Indian?'' Raider asked.

Clanton only laughed, his high-pitched tone piercing the stale night air.

CHAPTER THIRTEEN

Titus Tilden sat at his desk, gazing out onto Fifth Avenue. The street was alive with carriages and pedestrians moving back and forth in the glow of the gas lamps that lighted the avenue. Tilden had stayed late every day for a week. He had a man stationed at the Western Union office in case a message came in from Raider.

But there had been no telegram from Arizona. And on this particular evening, the messenger came back into the office shaking his head. Still no word from the big man.

Tilden leaned back in his chair, sighing. He had told Raider to check in at least once every two weeks. It had been almost a month since Raider had left Albuquerque for Adobe Sands. Not one communiqué had come in from the agency's most rambunctious operative.

Tilden rose from his desk, leaving behind the papers that could not hold his concentration. The slim, spectacled supervisor started for the front door until he realized that the lights were still on in Allan Pinkerton's office. Sometimes the head man shared an evening cup of coffee or tea with Wagner. Tilden was often invited to the informal meetings, so he did not think it out of line to knock on the door.

Pinkerton bade him enter.

Tilden sat down next to Wagner, who stirred a teacup.

"Coffee?" Pinkerton asked.

Tilden shook his head. "No, thank you, sir. I just wanted to ask you about something. A procedural matter."

Pinkerton nodded, but then said, "By the way, Titus, did

you see the letter of commendation from the Minnesota governor? He was pleased at the results of our investigation. The men wrapped up that swindler in two days' tin.e. Caught him red-handed trying to fleece a couple of farmers. Good choice on the assignment. You've come to know our agents well.''

"Too well," Tilden replied dolefully.

Wagner took notice of his assistant's tone. "Does this have anything to do with that case in Missouri?"

"The train holdups? No," Tilden replied. "I received a message from Stokes yesterday. They're on top of it."

Pinkerton eyed the young man. "A gang?"

Tilden shook his head. "They think it's an inside job. Stokes is on the trail of a former employee of the railroad. He's heading east. The man is believed to be hiding in Kentucky or Indiana."

Pinkerton nodded approvingly. "A good one, that Stokes. Never lets us down. Real steady."

Wagner took off his glasses, wiping them with a clean handkerchief. "Well," he said seriously, "if it isn't the Missouri thing, then it can only be Raider."

Tilden sighed. "Not a word from him since he left Albuquerque. I don't even know if he made it to Adobe Sands."

"He made it," Wagner replied.

Tilden looked at his bosses. "How can we be sure?"

Wagner shrugged. "If he was lying dead somewhere, someone would have discovered the body. He'd be carrying his credentials, and the local law agencies would have informed us."

"Pardon me, sir," Tilden offered, "but doesn't that ring of wishful thinking. I mean, the territories of New Mexico and Arizona are sizable, to say the least. What if he's lying dead where no one can find him?"

Pinkerton nodded and got up out of his chair. He looked at the map on the wall, putting his finger on Phoenix. "Do we have any men here?"

Tilden shook his head. "No. The closest man is in California. Sacramento to be exact."

Pinkerton sighed. "Too far away to do any good." He sat back down in his chair. "Too far," he repeated.

Wagner nodded in agreement. "It probably wouldn't do any

good to send anyone," he added. "Raider doesn't want a partner. He likes working alone. Which, quite frankly, I'm in favor of. If he works alone, then there's less of a chance that his partner will be killed in the crossfire."

Tilden thought that made sense, especially with Raider's predisposition toward using his Colt. "Still," he offered, "he could be in trouble. I admit that he's not as regular about messages as some of our other agents, but he usually is within a week of the time period that I appoint for him."

Pinkerton and Wagner both shifted in their chairs. Pinkerton poured himself a fresh cup of coffee. He stirred it and lifted it to his lips.

"I could get someone started in Raider's direction," Tilden offered. "Either the man in California, or someone in Texas. I could also notify the local authorities. The nearest town is Kingman. I believe they have a telegraph line in there. Now if Raider is—"

"That will be all, Titus."

He looked up to see Pinkerton glaring at him.

"But sir—"

"Leave it be, Titus," Wagner said. "Raider will be all right. If we haven't heard from him in a couple of weeks, we'll do our best to find him."

Tilden nodded and then, red-faced, excused himself.

He strode out of the office, into the cool air of the Chicago night. The wind was coming in off Lake Michigan, still warmed by the summer but hinting at the onrush of an early fall. He could not help but be baffled by the attitude of his superiors toward Raider. They left the rude, rough cowboy dangling by himself, almost as if they wished he would be killed, as if his demise would save them the trouble of dealing with him.

Tilden stopped under a gaslight. Could it be that he was starting to like Raider? He started walking again. No, he was just worried about him, the same way he worried about any agent who represented the Pinkerton name.

It was a professional concern. Nothing personal in it. Nothing to the nagging feeling that the big man was in trouble. Nothing at all.

CHAPTER FOURTEEN

Raider was not sure how many days he had been walking in the desert. He simply stumbled forward, bound with his wrists behind him, boots rubbing his feet raw. They had given him to the Indian. Pulido held the chain behind him, keeping a heathly distance so the big man could not attack him. The Mescalero had put chains on Raider's legs to keep his captive from running away.

Pulido also had Raider's Stetson, his Colt, and the black stallion.

"My doggie," the joker-faced Apache called. "We're going to El Dorado. Do you hear? El Dorado. Gold. A whole city of it."

At first, before Raider had lost track of the days, he had glared back at the skinny shaman, yelling at him, cursing him, accusing him of things that should have sent an Apache into a frenzy. But Pulido, Keeper of the Fangs and Talons, was different. He had no soul beyond his magic. His tribe had probably thrown him out, and the white man had been less than receptive. Pulido was a spook, a servant of the Devil himself.

"El Dorado. Do you know how many men have searched for it? Why, I have heard of it ever since the fathers taught me to speak English, when the mission was here." He laughed. "Now you will find it for me. Run little doggie."

He pulled the pistol and fired a shot at Raider's feet.

The big man did not flinch. He glanced back at the Indian with an animal gleam in his black eyes.

Pulido grew wide-eyed. "Move," he snapped. "Or I'll shoot you."

Raider measured the angle. Not right. Too much slack in the chain. The moment would come. Unless the little man killed him first. Then it did not matter. He turned back and started walking again.

They had passed into California. Of that he was almost sure. The ground was dead flat with hardly a tuft of greasewood as a sign of life. A sidewinder could live out here, but it would have to range far and wide to find a meal. Were they heading for Death Valley? Raider hated the desert. He had been lost once in the Mojave. It had almost killed him.

He was sure that he would die soon anyway. That's why he wanted to kill the Indian. It had to be right, though, for him to pull it off.

"El Dorado," the Mescalero kept saying. "It's out here somewhere. You will lead me to it, little doggie."

"Why don't you use my ass for a watering trough, you little rat-faced shithook!"

But the Indian only laughed.

They never stopped for long. Even at night, they weren't still for more than a couple of hours. The Indian could go a long time between naps. When they did sleep, Pulido would wrap the chain around Raider's body, locking it with strips of rawhide. Then he would make Raider lie down so he could pull off his boots. While the big man slept on the ground, the Mescalero curled up in Raider's bedroll.

That's okay, the big man kept telling himself. *When I get you, I ain't gonna let go. You're gonna be got.*

He'd wait until the time was right, or until Pulido tried to kill him.

They ate jerky and drank from a canteen. The Mescalero had also brought along two skins of water, as well as his clay jug full of loco-juice. Raider was sure that the Indian had laced his water with some sort of strange drug. His body felt the same stirring buzz it had known in the cave, just a little weaker. Trying to keep him confused.

"El Dorado!"

Pulido pointed in the distance.

Mountains rose up out of the plain. Raider did not know where the hell they were exactly. He kept walking, feeling the tension on his leash.

"Gold in those hills!" Pulido cried.

Sweat dripped down in Raider's eyes. As the peaks grew closer, he gazed upward, trying to find a landmark. They plodded forward, toward the base of the slopes.

They weren't in California, Raider thought. There were no mountains like these in California. He peered at the sun on his left. Were they going north? The damned potion had him all turned around. Maybe they had come northwest, into some of the lower ranges of Nevada.

As Raider stared at the mountains, Pulido jumped down from the saddle. He ran out a few paces in front of Raider, lifting his hands to the sky. Again he said the word he had been repeating: "El Dorado."

Raider's body tensed. He felt the right moment. Rush him. Knock him down. Stomp him to death.

He was a second late.

As he lunged forward, Pulido turned to see him coming. The Mescalero jumped to the side, avoiding the attack. Raider's weight carried him forward, and he fell in the dust.

Pulido cocked the Peacemaker and fired a shot within two inches of Raider's head. "Never again, white man. I will kill you the next time."

The Indian climbed back onto the horse. He dragged Raider for a few feet just to make his point. Then he allowed the big man to get up again. Raider, looking grimy and defeated, stumbled toward the slopes.

He was not broken. Not all the way. The Mescalero had taken most of it, but he could never destroy the spark of animal dignity that burned in Raider's gut. A wounded critter was the first one to turn and fight.

They followed the lower line of the mountains until they came to a pass that led back into the range.

Pulido held the gun on Raider while the big man drank from the canteen. The water tasted bitter, worse than before. His head began to spin almost immediately. Pulido was going to do it. He was going to kill him.

When he was back in the saddle, Pulido jerked the leash, urging Raider forward like a pack animal.

The sheer slopes of the pass rose to both sides. The path was barely big enough for the stallion. Raider kept his ears perked for the cocking hammer, the spinning cylinder of the Peacemaker. That had always seemed like the worse way to go, to be shot with your own gun.

"El Dorado!" the Indian cried.

Raider glanced over his shoulder to see the Mescalero raising the golden plate over his head.

When he looked back toward the slopes, he saw the gold reflection on the rock. A circle of the purest yellow jumped out of the mountain at him. A wall of gold. Raider shook his head. It was only a reflection. The loco-juice made it seem real.

Everything in his field of vision grew fuzzier. His legs weakened. But he kept going, watching the rocks, trying to concentrate on the tension of his chain leash.

"El Dorado!"

The echo pealed through the pass.

They turned a corner on the winding path.

Pulido cried out. He dropped the golden plate. The clanging echoed behind his scream. The Mescalero pointed toward the glittering wall ahead of them. Raider saw it too. A real wall of gold protruded from the rock. The biggest vein of gold he had ever seen.

His head throbbed, his chest heaved. Gold. To free him. All of it he could carry.

"El Dorado!" the Indian cried.

Freedom.

He felt the tightness of the chain. The Mescalero was standing in the stirrups, his eyes frozen on the shining tableau of ore. Now was the time, while the chain was wrapped around the little man's wrist.

Raider pulled with his torso, falling forward.

Pulido tumbled from the saddle of the black. He landed on his back, crying out in pain. Raider scrambled to his feet, stumbling toward the fallen Apache. He brought his heels down on his captor's head, stomping his skull, crying out with savage grunts.

The Indian stopped moving.

Raider staggered backward, looking down at Pulido. The big man shrieked a primitive cry of triumph that was fueled by the peyote concoction. He laughed loudly, shouting to the slopes.

He had killed the Mescalero.

Now the gold would be his.

He turned back toward the wall that glistened in the sun.

All his. A mountain of gold. He stumbled toward it, his hands still bound behind him.

"El Dorado," he muttered.

He collapsed there and did not wake up for the longest time.

When he opened his eyes, he was back in the cave. The torches burned all around him, along with the candles. A dim figure sat just out of the light, kneeling in the shadows.

Raider lifted his head. "Padre?"

Father Pedroza got up and moved next to him. "I have been praying for a week. But I knew you would not die. The Lord will not let you."

Raider fell back, his head hitting a soft roll of burlap. "No, He wouldn't kill me, but He'd sure let me go through some shit."

The padre crossed himself, mumbling some prayer.

"Sorry, padre," Raider offered. "I ain't feelin' so great."

He sure as hell didn't. Everything ached. He could not re-member what had happened. He wasn't sure he wanted to. He did recall Thornton and Clanton giving him to the Indian. And the gold. El Dorado.

"Sleep," the padre said. "I'll get you something to eat. Here, drink. Go on. It's not the peyote the Mescalero was giving you."

The padre had to lift the big man's head to help him drink the cool water.

"What happened to the Indian?" Raider asked.

The padre lowered his head. "You killed him. I saw it all. I was following you the whole time. Pulido led you in circles and brought you back to the mountains just north of here. He was going to kill you until he saw that—"

"Gold," Raider muttered. "I got to go back there. I got to see it."

When he tried to sit up, the padre urged him back down. "You are too weak. You must get your strength back. Then you must do what you came here to do."

Raider grunted. "What was it I came here to do?"

"To bring the men in Adobe Sands to justice."

"Sure, padre. I'll do it tomorrow."

But tomorrow lasted for a while. Raider slept a lot, waking only to drink and eat. The padre brought him meat and bread and water. Raider did not even think to ask him where he was getting it.

His skin peeled off from the sun he had gotten during his walk in the desert. Pedroza brought him a salve to heal the blotches. Raider just lay there as the padre tended his wounds. His black eyes stared off into the shadows. There was no expression on his face, just blankness.

Almost a week had passed and the big man had not said a word. Father Pedroza started to worry. He had seen strong men become soulless under extreme conditions. Was Raider the kind to be destroyed inside?

"Why didn't you stop the Mescalero?" Raider asked one day. "Why didn't you help me?"

Pedroza crossed himself. "I would have been forced to kill him. He would not have given up without a fight. I cannot take a life, señor. I am a man of God. I waited for Him to deliver you, which He has done."

The next day Raider stood up for the first time. He wobbled a little, but he was able to walk. He stretched, feeling his body, making sure nothing had been damaged permanently.

That evening, the padre made a pot of stew from the meat and potatoes brought to him by those few remaining sodbusters who made confession.

Raider looked up from his bowl, staring right through Pedroza. "Where's the nearest telegraph office?" he asked.

"Kingman. Will we go there tomorrow?"

Raider shook his head. "When I'm stronger."

Three days later, the big man stood at the mouth of the cave, looking out at the high clouds in the blue sky. "I'm gonna need my horse, padre. And my gun."

"I have them," Pedroza replied. "Shall I get them now?"

"No." He worked the fingers of his gun hand. "I got to ask you some questions first. And I also want you to listen. Since my head cleared up, a lot of things come back to me. I want you to help me figure it out."

They sat until evening, talking over the fire. Pedroza was a smart man and a good listener. He kept nodding as the big man ironed out the details that had bothered him so much before.

"You have solved the mystery, señor," Pedroza said finally. "Now you must arrest Thornton and his men."

"Not yet.'

Pedroza frowned. "What do you mean?"

Raider had a half smirk on his face. "I want to catch them. To lay a trap. To feel the satisfaction of seein' their faces when I spring it on 'em. I got that comin', padre."

"If the Lord wills it."

Raider did not reply. He did not want to mess with the Lord. He just wanted to set the snare, the way he had done hundreds of times before.

"Tomorrow I go Kingman," Raider said finally. "I got to send a message and buy some dynamite."

Pedroza suddenly had a funny look in his eyes.

"Somethin' eatin' you, padre?"

"Señor. I will help you any way I can., But please, do not ask me to kill. I cannot. I have never killed a living thing."

Raider's eyes narrowed. "I stood right here and watched you shoot that mescalero's pet snake. You blew its head off with one shot."

Pedroza shook his head, an expression of disbelief on his pious countenance. "No, señor. You are wrong. I did not kill the snake. It was dead when I got back. I thought you killed it."

Raider grinned and slapped him on the shoulder. "Thank you, padre. I think you just told me somethin' I needed to know. The last piece of the puzzle."

Pedroza was not sure what Raider meant. "I wish you had some men to fight with you. The homesteaders are too weak. And my drunken brother has disappeared. I cannot find his worthless hide anywhere."

"Don't worry," the big man replied. "He'll turn up."

Raider was beginning to feel more like himself.

"What else do you need, señor?"

Raider thought about it. "My saddlebags still on the black?"

"*Sí.*"

"I hope that Apache weasel didn't throw everything away. Although I might be able to remember it if I try hard enough. The message has to be sent to the right people for it to work."

The padre still looked worried. "Señor, I wish I could help you. But as I said, I cannot kill. No matter what they say about me."

Raider nodded sympathetically. "I know, padre. But don't fret. I'll take care of any killin' that's needed. And don't hold it agin me if there's a lot of it."

"I'll pray for you, señor."

"You do that," the big man replied., "And tell the Man upstairs to give me a break this time."

The next day, Raider rode into Kingman to send his messages.

Then, using the Mescalero's golden plate for barter, he purchased dynamite and cartridges for his Colt and his Winchester.

When he was outfitted, he went to the sheriff in an attempt to raise a posse. The lawman did not want to get involved. Adobe Sands was out of his jurisdiction. Even if he wanted to help, it wouldn't be legal. As far as the sheriff was concerned, the Pinkerton was flat-out on his own.

Raider thanked him and started back to Adobe Sands.

CHAPTER FIFTEEN

The sun was sinking behind Raider and the padre. Raider lay prone on the rise, gazing in the direction of the barracks where Clanton and his men stayed on the outskirts of Adobe Sands. The padre eyed the case of dynamite, wringing his hands in a perpetual nervous motion. He stepped back when Raider scooted down the incline.

"Señor, do you really need all this?" The priest began to pace back and forth. "Must you deal out death so carelessly?"

Raider withdrew the knife from his boot, slipping the blade under the slats on top of the dynamite box. "Padre, I plan to be real careful. Only thing is, with you too scared to help me, I'm gonna need somebody else when things get hot. Another hand if I'm gonna pull it off."

The padre grimaced. "I am not scared, señor. I simply do not wish to kill anyone."

Raider started to tie the dynamite in bundles of three sticks. "Then leave all that to me. Just try to rustle up another person."

"The homesteaders are too scared," Pedroza replied. "And there aren't many of them left anyway. The ones who are here are too far away for Thornton to concern himself. It would not be good for him to buy their land, so he does not bother with them. Nor do they bother him."

The padre watched as Raider continued to work in silence. The big man tied bundles in the diminishing light. It was dark by the the time he had the ten charges ready. The padre jumped back when Raider started to wedge the fuses into the red explosives.

"Don't fret," Raider said. "They won't explode till somebody lights them. Then . . . *boom!*" He gave a little laugh.

Pedroza shook his head. "How can you take so much pleasure in killing, Señor Raider? You are a good man. You should know that all the evil in the world cannot be killed."

"Well, you may not be able to kill it all, but you can sure as hell try, padre." Raider threaded his arm through a coiled line of fuse. "It's dark enough. Sit tight. I'll be back."

He gathered up the charges and put them in a burlap sack.

"Be careful," Pedroza called, crossing himself.

Raider started out toward the barracks. It was a long building, narrow like a covered bridge. The big man knew from his observations that Clanton's remaining cutthroats took supper about dark every day. They were all sitting around the dinner table, spooning stew into their hungry mouths. Raider planned on shutting a few of their yaps. For all the sodbusters, for Carrie and her father, for himself.

Laughter rose from the bunkhouse. Probably having a few shots of whiskey to make their dinner go down easy. Raider slipped up to the wall and dropped to his belly. He found ample crawl space under the bunkhouse, tossing a few rocks underneath in case any rattlesnakes were hiding in the darkness.

No one heard him as he set the charges. He linked them all together with the length of fuse, securing the ends of the fuse line at the edge of the barracks where they could both be lit at the same time. When he was finished, he scooted out from under the house and ran back toward the ridge.

The padre came out of the shadows. "I did not hear an explosion."

"You won't for a while," Raider replied.

"But . . ."

"One thing you got to learn, padre. When you're playin' poker, you can't force your hand too early. You got to play it out to the end and make the timin' just right." He gazed back toward Adobe Sands. "Them boys is all at the card table, raisin' on every bet like they got a pat hand. Only I'm gonna stay right with 'em till I show my straight flush."

"You talk in riddles, señor."

Raider started toward the rock where the stallion was tied.

"Come on, boy. Let's get into position. We may have another few days of watchin' on our hands. It'll take at least three, maybe four days for the others to get here from Phoenix."

Pedroza nodded and started after him.

Raider planned to set up on a spot where he could watch the southeast approach to Adobe Sands.

The padre understood, even though he was not sure the plan would work.

As they made their way through the night, the padre noticed that Raider kept looking over his shoulder, to the rear.

"What is it, señor?" Pedroza asked.

"Shh." Raider handed him the reins of the black. "Just keep walkin'. I'm gonna surprise whoever it is that's followin' us."

When Pedroza was gone, Raider eased back into the darkness. It wasn't long before he heard the scuffling feet on the sand. As the figure drew closer, he dived from the shadows and wrestled him to the ground.

"No, señor!" the man cried. "Please, do not hurt me."

Raider stood up, drawing his Colt. "Diego. Where the devil did you come from? Father Pedroza, get on back here. It's your brother."

The shiftless Diego rose to his feet, brushing himself off.

His pious brother came running back with the stallion behind him. "Diego, where have you been? I was worried sick about you."

Diego lowered his head. "I was ashamed of myself. I have been hiding. The sun has baked all the tequila out of me. No longer do I use the Mescalero herbs. My head is clear. I want to help."

Raider eyed the Spaniard, who was almost a dead ringer for his brother. "I bet you do want to help. You done plenty already."

Diego gaped at the big man. "What do you mean?"

Raider laughed. "You know what the hell I mean. Only it don't matter now. If you come to help, I got somethin' you can do."

Diego nodded. "Anything."

"You ever light a fuse before?" Raider asked.

"No," Diego replied.

Raider took a match out of his shirt pocket. "Ain't much to it. Just one strike and a touch. Then . . ."

Diego took the match. "I know. Where is this fuse?"

"On the bunkhouse at the northwest corner. Two of them. Think you can handle it?"

Diego smiled. "*Sí.* But I should have more than one match."

"You're catchin' on, Diego. Come on, go with us. We're gonna do some watchin' and then we're gonna do my plan. I'll fill you in on the whole thing when we're settled."

Diego extended his hand. "I will not let you down."

Raider shook hands with him. "No, I don't reckon you will."

Father Pedroza was staring at both of them as if he did not approve. "I wish you were not so eager to help him kill other men, Diego. It proves what I have known about your soul."

"God will guide us all," came his brother's reply.

Raider wasn't sure that God even cared that much about the workings of three desperate men. He liked to think his Maker was on his side. But if the timing wasn't right, even the big Man upstairs couldn't do much to help them.

The August sun was merciless. There was no shade where they waited, watching to the southeast. Father Pedroza, who baked under his cassock, paced nervously back and forth. His brother sat diligently beside Raider, keeping his eyes on the horizon.

"Waiting and waiting," the padre said. "If they were going to come, they would be here by now."

Raider shook his head. "Not necessarily. It's a long way from Phoenix. They'll be coming by coach, probably. The roads ain't that good."

The padre reached for the water bottle. "I do not feel right about this. This scheme is too risky."

Raider turned around and pointed a finger at Pedroza. "Now look here, padre. I know you're a man of the cloth and all that. But I've about had it with your bellyachin'. If you don't like the way things are goin', you can just clear out. Comprende?"

Pedroza's face grew red, but he was quiet thereafter.

Raider glanced at Diego. "I didn't mean to talk so nasty to

him, but he ain't shut up for three days.''

Diego nodded. "He has been that way since we were children. He knows nothing of guns. He is afraid of them."

"You afraid of guns, Diego?" the big man asked.

The padre's brother eyed Raider cautiously. "What do you mean?"

Without a word of warning, Raider drew his colt and tossed it to Diego. The Spaniard caught the Colt by the butt and twirled it on his finger. He handed it back to Raider, butt first.

"I learned to shoot in the Army," he said.

Raider nodded, holstering the weapon. "I bet you did. Diego, when this thing is over, you and me have to talk."

He squinted at Raider. "Sí I will talk."

Father Pedroza looked up a them. "You're both talking in riddles now."

Diego glared back at his brother. "Jesus talked in parables, Amerigo. And when he saw the moneylenders in the temple, he drove them out with a whip. Righteous indignation."

Father Pedroza only scoffed, hurrying away to say prayers for them.

Diego smiled. "He hates it that I know the Bible almost as well as he does. He resents me, but he does not know what it is like to lose your wife and child. He does not know what that does to a man."

"What was that again?" Raider asked. "Righteous . . . what?"

"Righteous indignation," Diego replied.

Raider grinned. Righteous indignation. He liked the sound of it.

Raider was at the water jug when he heard Diego screaming. He ran up to the crest of the ridge and looked toward the horizon. Dust rose up from the plain, a big, thick cloud, probably from a coach.

"Is this what you have been waiting for?" Diego asked.

Raider nodded. "Maybe."

He looked up at the sky. It was late afternoon. Perfect. The oncoming coach could not be more than thirty minutes away.

Raider lifted the Colt from his holster, checking the cylinder.

Five shots. He took the sixth cartridge from his belt and filled the empty chamber.

Below them, the padre crossed himself. "More killing. I will pray for the souls of all involved."

Raider started down the incline, toward the stallion. "Give me until dark, Diego. And then light them fuses. Got it?"

Diego nodded. "At dark, señor!"

Raider swung into the saddle. "This is it, boys. What you might call the moment of truth, padre. If we fail, everything is wasted. And all them sodbusters died for no reason."

The padre looked like he was ready to get cranked up with some quote from the Good Book. But Raider never heard it. He spurred the black, driving for the dusty ghost town of Adobe Sands.

He circled around, coming in the back way. Things were quiet, so nobody noticed as he tied the black to the rain gutter behind the general store. He climbed to the top of the building and crawled to the edge to look over the parapet. The coach drew nearer, barreling down the main street into town.

Three men got out at the hotel. Just as he had expected. Raider looked up at the sky. He had to move quickly. He had to get into the hotel before Diego set off the fireworks. And he had to get inside without anyone seeing him.

CHAPTER SIXTEEN

Raider eased next to the window of Adrian Thornton's bedroom on the first floor of the hotel. He could hear voices inside. They were in the lobby, the visitors inquiring, Thornton welcoming them. Raider tried the window and found it open. He slipped in, holding his Colt in front of him.

The bedroom door was closed. He stood next to the threshold, trying to make out what they were saying. He couldn't hear the words, only the tones. The visitors sounded disturbed.

Helen Mallory's voice rose above the rest. "Adrian, take them into your office. I'll see to it that you have drinks and refreshments. Would you gentlemen care for some fine whiskey? I'll just be a moment. Go on, Adrian. Make them feel at home. They've come all this way."

The bedroom door swung open. She gasped when she saw Raider standing there. He grabbed her and put his hand over her mouth.

"Are you with me or agin me?" he whispered.

She nodded. He took his hand off her mouth and looked at her face. There was still a bruise on her cheek where Clanton had slapped her.

She closed the door and put her arms around his neck. "Clanton said you were dead. How did you—"

Raider drew back. "There ain't time. Just keep out of the way while I face these boys."

She put her hand on his chest. "Raider, I'll stay quiet. But you got to help me get out of here, one way or another."

He nodded. "Now get to the saloon and stay there no matter what you see or hear."

She kissed him for luck.

Raider hugged the wall, easing down the corridor toward Thornton's office. The door was open. He could hear them talking inside.

"But I never called you here," Thornton was saying. "It's a mistake, Mr. McPeters. I never—"

A voice boomed over Thornton's nasal inflection. "All three of us received the same telegram in Phoenix. It says, 'Trouble. Come at once or the whole deal is over.' And your name was at the bottom. We come all this way and now you tell us that you didn't send this."

"No, I didn't," Thornton insisted.

"Who did?"

Raider squared himself in the doorway of the office. "I did, gentlemen. I wanted to see you personally, to tell you what's goin' on around here."

Three faces gaped at him. Thornton moved toward his desk. Raider thumbed the hammer of the Peacemaker.

"Don't do it, Adrian." He waved the barrel. "Why don't you just sit over there next to your bosses."

Thornton moved away from his desk, sidling next to a round, red-faced man in a brown suit. The man was balding, with bushy eyebrows and a bulbous nose. He glared at Raider with steely, bloodshot eyes.

The big Pinkerton came into the room and closed the door behind him. "You must be Mr. McPeters," he said to the red-faced man. Then, regarding the other two, "The Benedict brothers. I see the family resemblance."

McPeters scowled at Raider. "Who the hell are you?"

Raider tipped back his Stetson with the barrel of the Colt. "I'm the Pinkerton agent that was sent in here to find out what the hell was going on with the padre. Adrian there called me in."

McPeters turned his ire on his associate. "You did what, Adrian?"

Thornton cowered against the wall. "I thought the priest was going to kill all of us. He was shooting down our men like they were nothing."

"The padre wasn't shootin' nobody," Raider said.

Thornton glared at him. "Lies. He was behind everything."

Raider shook his head. "Nope, but we're tryin' to saddle a

mustang while he's movin'. Don't get too far ahead till we tell your bosses here what's really been goin' on.''

The Benedict brothers whispered to one another. They were ratty-looking, like prairie dogs that couldn't find enough to eat. Raider ignored them, keeping his eyes on McPeters.

"You boys is buyin' up this land so you can resell it to the railroad,'' he offered. "Ain't you?''

McPeters's chest swelled. "There's no law against that.''

Raider waved the Colt. "Yeah, but there is a law against killin' people, against burnin' them out so they'll leave.''

One of the Benedict brothers stood up. "What are you talking about?'' he said. "We never told anyone to force out the home-steaders.''

"That's right,'' the other brother rejoined. "We felt they had just as much right to speculate and take their chances.''

"Somebody else didn't feel that way,'' Raider replied. "Family name of the Youngbloods had their house burned to the ground. And a few weeks back, the Calders were killed and their roof set on fire. If you don't believe me, I can take you to the place where they are buried. I put them in the ground myself.''

McPeters wheeled toward Thornton. "You! You're behind all this. You're the one who'll go to the gallows.''

Thornton trembled before his boss. "No, I never . . . I told Clanton not to use force. I made it clear.''

"Not clear enough,'' McPeters growled.

Raider swung around behind Thornton's desk. "Don't go placin' the blame just yet,'' the big man said. "We got more talkin'.''

McPeters's eyes narrowed. "What are you saying?''

Raider nodded at Adrian Thornton. "Ole Thorny there is tellin' the truth, or at least half of it.''

Thornton stared in disbelief at Raider. "You believe me?''

"I do.'' He smiled. "You see, I got to thinkin' about it. I mean, why would Thornton call me in to hunt down the padre if he was the one behind all the attacks on the homesteaders? No, even a dim candle like Thornton wouldn't be that stupid.''

Thornton frowned at the remark.

"Adrian really thought he was callin' in the troops,'' Raider continued. "Clanton couldn't find Pedroza, even though Ace was buddyin' around with the Mescalero named Pulido. Clanton told Pulido to help get rid of me, only it didn't work.''

McPeters sat down, folding his arms. ''Hollow accusations.''

Raider took off his hat and set it on the desk. ''Think so?'' He pulled something out of the Stetson and threw it at McPeters. ''Mescalero charms. Found on the ground each time one of your men was murdered by the so-called padre. Clanton planted them there to confuse ever'body and make them think the padre was hooked up with the Apache. I even believed it myself for a while.''

Thornton spoke up. ''But you just admitted that the padre did the shooting. Isn't that right?''

''Not exactly,'' the big man replied. ''It was somebody masqueradin' as the padre. A couple of 'em. You see, Clanton was the one who tried to shoot me the night I got here. He found a robe, probably when he burned down the church. He also put on the robe the day he attacked the Calders with his men. Wanted ever'one to think the padre had turned against the sodbusters. Couldn't resist dressin' up like Pedroza.''

''Are you telling me Clanton shot his own men?'' Thornton asked.

Raider shook his head. ''No. But I'll get to that in a minute. Right now I want to stay on Clanton.''

McPeters and the Benedict brothers had their eyes on him.

Raider came around and leaned back on the desk. ''Clanton was the one behind the attacks on the sodbusters. I thought for a while that Thornton knew about the raids, but then I figured he wouldn't be callin' me in if he was part of the plan.'' He looked at Adrian Thornton., ''How'd Clanton take it when you told him that you was bringin' in a Pinkerton, Thorny?''

''Why, he was against it,'' Thornton replied. ''Told me that he could handle everything.''

Raider nodded. ''I figured as much. Clanton wanted to take me when I first got to town. But he knew I was too fast. So he planned to take me away from town. Get me headin' in the wrong direction and send his man Pulido to do the dirty work. Killin' me right out wouldn't do the job. I had to disappear so if anybody came lookin' for me, it didn't seem like I had been bushwhacked. I think they planned to tell some story about me lookin' for El Dorado. But it wouldn't matter by that time, 'cause all the sodbusters woulda been gone.''

McPeters leered at the smiling detective. "You don't seem like the kind of man who's capable of such thinking."

Raider chuckled sarcastically. "Oh, I been thinkin' a lot, McPeters. See, I figured if Clanton wasn't answerin' to Thornton here, then who was he answerin' to? Who was payin' for the gang on the edge of town? Thorny sure as hell didn't have that much money.''

"That's right!" Thornton rejoined. "I never gave Ace Clanton a red cent beyond his own pay. When I asked about his men, he said that it didn't matter. He told me the men would stay out of their loyalty to him."

Raider's eyes narrowed in a pitying expression. "And you believed that? Hell, no wonder Clanton didn't have any trouble foolin' you. You took the fall, Thornton. The front man who didn't suspect a thing."

"Balderdash!" McPeters cried. "This sounds more like a story from some penny novel."

Raider glanced toward the fading light on the window. "Gonna be dark soon. Maybe we oughta fire up a lamp."

He struck a match and torched the wick of a lamp that sat on Thornton's desk. "That's better. Now I can see your face, Mr. McPeters."

The rotund gentleman stood up. "I don't know about you gentlemen, but I'm not going to sit here another moment while this ruffian—"

Raider put the barrel of the Colt in his chest. "Just sit down, Mac. We ain't finished yet."

McPeters was red as a beet as he eased back onto the wooden chair.

Raider grinned. "That's better. Now where was I? Oh yeah, Clanton's boss. The three of you? Or just one? That's the last question. How many of you knowed about Clanton?"

The Benedict brothers looked at each other and then at McPeters.

Raider nodded. "I thought so. The one who yells the loudest is always the one with his finger in the gravy."

McPeters grunted. "You can't prove a thing."

One of the Benedicts spoke up. "You were the one who insisted on hiring Clanton, Alexander. My brother and I were opposed to it because of his familial connection to the infamous Ike Clanton. We felt he would not be the sort of man who we would like to have associated with this project."

Raider grinned at McPeters. "How 'bout it, Mac? You gonna come clean?"

McPeters sighed. "All right. I was the one who hired Clanton. But I never told him to kill anyone."

"I don't believe that," Raider said.

McPeters leaned forward, a penitent look in his eyes—the look of a man who's sorry after he's been caught. "We're all reasonable men here. A deal. That's what we need. How much, Pinkerton? How much do you want?"

Raider shook his head. He was going to decline. To dress down the fat, red-faced man.

But the voice came behind him. "No deals."

Raider wheeled toward the window to see Ace Clanton holding a scattergun on him.

"Drop it, big man," Clanton said. "Go on."

Raider hesitated with the Colt in his hand. He could chance it. But if Clanton fired, he would cut him in half.

"You ain't gonna shoot," the big man bluffed. "You might hit your boss."

"Try me," the scar-faced man replied. "I don't want to kill all of you, but I will if I have to."

McPeters reached around and grabbed the Colt out of Raider's hand. "Good work, Clanton. I'll cover him while you come in."

McPeters made Raider back off as Clanton climbed through the window.

"Got you now, big man," Ace said. "I was listenin' outside the whole time. You know, you're a lot smarter than you look."

With his hands in the air, Raider wasn't sure how smart he was.

CHAPTER SEVENTEEN

Alexander McPeters held the Colt in his right hand, waving everyone but Clanton back against the wall. "You too, Pinkerton."

Raider fell in beside Thornton and the Benedict brothers.

McPeters scowled at his subordinate. "Thornton, you idiot, this is all your doing. If you hadn't been such a coward, you wouldn't have called in this big tub of guts."

"You're the tub of guts!" Raider offered.

McPeters bristled. "I'll get to you later." He looked back at Thornton. "You've ruined everything, you Yankee dimwit."

Thornton started edging toward the office door. "I'm leaving," he said in a quavering voice. "I don't care what you've done. I won't tell anyone. I swear to God."

McPeter's face went slack. "No, you won't tell anyone."

The Colt exploded, deafening them in the confines of the small room. Thornton slumped to the floor, holding his chest. Blood gushed between his fingers. Raider leaned forward, but Clanton urged him back with the scattergun.

"That's far enough, big 'un." He grinned at Raider. "Somethin', huh, how you got away from that Injun. You kill him?"

Raider smiled back. "I stomped him a little."

McPeters wheeled around with the Colt. He regarded his partners, the Benedict brothers. "Gentlemen, we have come to the moment of decision. You know the truth. I intimidated the homesteaders through Clanton here. I freely admit it. You can stay with me, or you can . . . well, you understand."

Both of them shook their heads. They could not be with him. McPeters sighed and waved the barrel of Raider's Colt.

"Take them outside," the fat man ordered.

"What are you going to do to us?" asked one of the brothers.

Clanton flashed his brown-toothed grin. "Gonna have a little coach accident. Plenty of dropoffs around here. Be a shame if that pretty wagon outside fell into one of 'em."

"Be a shame if you fell with it," Raider said.

"Mighty cocky," Clanton replied. "Come on, let's go. You two brothers first. I want the big man where I can keep the shotgun barrels in his back."

With the Benedicts in front of him, Raider moved slowly through the corridor, into the lobby and out the front door. Clanton kept cold iron in his back. One trip of the triggers and his torso would be gone.

As soon as he was outside, Raider turned west. The sun was only an orange sliver, peeking over the mountains with one last wink before it disappeared for good. Almost dark. If it was going to happen, it would be soon. One match, a tiny lick of flame touched to a pair of fuses. The bunkhouse would be gone, and the distraction might just be enough for the big man to make a move—possibly his last.

He looked toward the northern edge of town. "Come on, Diego."

Ace Clanton stood by the team of horses that pulled McPeters's four-seater coach. "What are you talkin' about, Pink?"

"Kiss my ass, Clanton."

The scar-faced outlaw shook his head. "Dang me if you ain't about the toughest one I ever seen. Shame to kill you." He took a pair of manacles from his gunbelt. "Turn around. Hands behind your back."

Raider grimaced. "Ain't no need for that."

Clanton chortled. "You think I'm stupid enough to let you keep your hands free? Turn around."

He hesitated, trying to stall, peering anxiously over Clanton's shoulder toward the edge of town. "Ain't you even gonna let me die the way I want?"

The sun was gone.

McPeters came outside now, lighting the lamps on the side of the coach.

Raider wondered if Diego had the gumption. You never knew what was in a man's guts until he had to follow through for you. What if the Spaniard had gone back to the tequila bottle?

Raider turned, putting his hands behind him.

"Yeah," Clanton repeated. "It's a shame to have to kill you."

Raider squirmed so the manacle wouldn't go on. "You might be the one who gets killed, Ace. Strange things can happen sometimes."

"Hold that hand still. I can't—"

The explosion lit up the dusky sky, shaking the ground, sending shock waves through the air.

When Clanton turned toward the fireball, Raider swung his hand around, catching the outlaw with a stiff backhand.

As Clanton went down, McPeters leveled the Peacemaker at Raider. The Benedict brothers charged their former partner, knocking him to the ground. The Colt went off harmlessly, sending a slug toward the heavens.

"Get in the coach!" Raider yelled at the Benedicts.

They climbed in as the big man jumped up to the driver's seat. He loosened the brake and shook the reins, urging the team forward, driving toward the source of the explosion. Clanton jumped up, quickly unleashing both barrels of the scattergun. The shot bounced off the backside of the four-seater.

Raider turned when he had cleared the general store, making due west. They'd come after him, or at least Clanton would. The bunkhouse was gone now, so there wouldn't be any men to help him.

The wind rushed by Raider's face.

"Good boy, Diego," he said to himself.

But then, after what he had figured out about the padre's brother, he had been almost certain that Diego would not let him down.

When Raider reached the Calder spread, he halted the team. All four animals were lathered in the heat of the summer night.

Raider stood up in the driver's seat, gazing back east. He expected to see torches coming. Even on the hard ground, the tracks of the coach would be easy to spot.

He climbed down and opened the coach door. The Benedicts were clinging to the seats. The ride had scared the hell out of them.

"Come on, boys, we ain't got much time."

They got out slowly, asking Raider what he planned to do.

The big man moved forward and started to unhitch three of the team horses. "We're climbin'," he said. "I just hope I can find the way in the dark. You boys know how to ride?"

They both nodded.

"Let's go."

Riding bareback, they started along the Little Sands. There wouldn't be a moon until later. Raider wondered if Clanton would follow him in the dark. If the scar-faced man had been working with Pulido, then there was a good chance he knew the mountains pretty well.

They moved into the hills, climbing on the narrow path. When they were on a high point, Raider looked back. Two torches burned like tiny dots of yellow in the distance. Clanton and McPeters? Maybe the dynamite hadn't gotten all of Clanton's men.

One of the brothers asked him what he was looking at.

"Just keep goin'," he replied.

But the path was slow in the dark. They came down into the valley where the Youngbloods' house had been burned to the ground. Raider scraped around for something to make a torch. He tore a sleeve from his shirt and wrapped it on the stub of a charcoaled beam. But it never burned. No one had a match, and there were no flint rocks to make a spark.

One of the Benedicts gasped. He pointed back toward the hills. The torches were right behind them.

"What do we do now?"

Raider pointed at the dark cliffs overhead. "We keep climbing."

They made for the slopes, abandoning the horses when their hooves began slipping on the sandstone. Both of the brothers were breathing hard. One of them had a hand to his chest.

"Don't give up on me," the big man urged. "I gotta say I was proud of the way you stood up to McPeters. You coulda gone along with him and saved your hides. But you sure as hell didn't."

One of them replied that the Benedicts had always enjoyed a reputation for being honest. They could not risk losing that reputation, even if it meant facing death. The family honor was important above all.

Raider exhaled. "You boys ain't from Arkansas, are you?"

They weren't. Raider looked back down the mountain. The torches were at the ruins of the homestead.

The big man glanced up again. Were they close to the spot where he had first seen the padre? Maybe Diego and his brother were searching for them in the hills. He sure wished he had a gun.

"All right," he said, "this is the way it stands. I want both of you to climb. Just keep goin'. You may run into the padre. No, don't worry, he ain't gonna kill you. Just tell him the story if you see him. All of it. And tell him I'm gonna be down here tryin' to ambush Clanton and whoever came with him."

"What if we don't find the padre?"

Raider shrugged. "There may be a cave up there where you can hide. Or you can climb on down to the other side. If you're lucky, you'll find somebody to help you. If not, don't worry about it."

"We'll be dead."

"Just climb, damn it."

They shook his hand and started upward.

Raider turned toward the torches again. They were heading straight for the mountain. Raider picked up a rock. Not much firepower against a scattergun. He wondered if somebody down there had his Colt.

He began to climb himself, but in another direction. He planned to move among the big boulders at the top, where the padre had been that day. He might be able to keep them from finding him and at the same time harass them enough to let the Benedicts get away. They had a chance if they ran into the padre. Otherwise the honest, ratty-looking gentlemen would be buzzard bait.

Raider squared off in the high boulders and watched as the torches glided toward him.

They were good trackers. Clanton seemed to be finding every scrape and nick in the rocks. At one point, the torches were together, flickering over the same spot. Then one of them went out, leaving only the single flame to light the way.

Raider held the rock in his hands. "Come on," he muttered. "Find me if you think you can."

The torch looked long and hard, burning until the moon was in the sky. Raider peered up at the lonely crescent. It would be enough light. His ears could do the rest.

Apparently his pursuers felt the same way. The second torch flickered and died. He could not see them now, but they could not see him either. He listened as boots scraped on stone.

Somebody was getting closer. Raider leaned over the boulder to peer down at the path. He could see the outline coming toward him. A felt hat caught the rays of the moon.

Just a few more steps, the big man told himself.

A spectral face turned upward into the moonglow.

Raider lifted the rock over his head.

The face turned down to look at the path.

Raider hurled the rock with everything he had.

An echo of crunching bone in the night air. The body slumped to the ground. Raider waited for the other one to fire. Nothing. He peered down at the body, thinking the two of them must have split up. If he could just get to the fallen man's gun.

He eased down the slope, hovering over the body.

The light wasn't bright, but he could tell that the man was not Clanton. No scar. Not McPeters. Too thin. Maybe all of Clanton's help had not gone up with the bunkhouse. He was dead now, though.

Raider began to feel around for the man's weapon. He froze when he heard the chinking sound of a pistol cylinder. A Colt erupted in the rocks below him, sending chunks of lead that barely missed his skull. Raider hurried back up the incline with the gunfire chasing him.

"I'm gonna get you, Pinkerton," Ace Clanton cried. "I'm gonna kill you if it takes all night."

Raider was going to do his best to take him the distance. He made for the highest peaks, wondering if he was close to the cave where he had hidden with the padre and the Mescalero. His heart skipped a beat when he saw the glow from above. Only torches inside a cave could make that kind of eerie light.

He found handholds in a sheer cliff. When he rolled over onto the ledge, he saw the mouth of the cave. He went in to find the Benedict brothers huddled together. They looked scared half to death.

"We heard shooting."

Raider started back for the mouth of the cave. "You're liable to hear a lot more."

Scuffling on the ledge outside the mouth of the cave. Clanton was already up. And if he checked his partner's body, he probably knew that Raider did not have a gun.

Clanton's ragged face looked in from the entrance.

Raider pushed the Benedicts back. He took one of the torches from the cave wall. When Clanton stepped toward them, Raider flung the torch at him. Clanton stepped aside and grinned.

"You're a goner now, big man. I gotta say that you're the toughest man I ever had to kill." He cocked the Colt—Raider's own weapon—and took careful aim. "Goodbye, Pinkerton."

Raider heard the rattling from the shadows. Clanton heard it too. A long, squirming shape fluttered out of the dark recess of the cave. It wrapped around Clanton's neck. He screamed, trying to pull it off.

It was bigger than Pulido's rattlesnake. The wide mouth popped open, then struck three-inch fangs into Clanton's face. He finally managed to fling it off, pumping two shots straight into the snake's head. The reptile squirmed to a violent death on the cave floor.

Clanton staggered backward, holding his face. "Help me," he cried. "Do somethin'. Don't let me die."

Raider started for him, but it was too late. Clanton staggered onto the ledge, balancing on the rock. The rattler had blinded him. He took one too many steps and fell off the ledge, slamming on the rocks below.

Raider looked stunned, but muttered, "Sorry I let you die, Ace."

A shape eased from the recesses of the cave. A man in a cassock. Raider nodded at him.

"I'm gonna take care of the Benedicts," the big man said. "Get me some water and some of that tequila if there's any around.

The hooded figure nodded back. Raider could not see his face. He turned to regard the brothers, both of whom seemed to be holding up well.

"We ain't dead yet, are we, boys?" He looked back toward the entrance of the cave. "Pedroza, where'd you get that other snake? Pedroza?"

The cowled man had fled. Raider heard him scuffling down the cliff, his hands struggling for purchase. It didn't matter. Raider had to get back into town and arrest Alexander McPeters.

He grimaced at the Benedicts. "You boys ready for some more action?"

They both nodded and asked if they could sleep for a while.

Raider told them that everything could wait until morning. He wanted to take a little nap himself. And if they were hungry, they could make a fire and roast up the rattlesnake. It was plenty big enough to feed them all.

CHAPTER EIGHTEEN

"Just keep them steady, Benedict. Hold tight on the reins. I want to go slow-like. You understand?"

A nod from the wide-eyed driver, Matt or David Benedict. Raider did not know which one he was. He hadn't relished the idea of putting on the dead man's clothes, so he would look like Clanton's assistant. Raider sat on the driver's seat of the coach, his hands wrapped loosely in rope so it would appear that he had been bound after his imminent capture.

In the back, the body of Clanton sat propped up with a stick, so it would appear that he was a passenger in the coach. The other dead man, clad in David or Matt Benedict's clothes, lay on the floor face down. They had spent all morning rounding up horses and making the necessary adjustments for their entrance. Raider wanted it to look like Clanton had been success-ful, in case there were any of Clanton's men who had not been killed in the explosion. He wanted a quiet ride down the main street.

"Right up next to the hotel door," Raider said.

Benedict was pretty good at handling the team. He braked in front of the hotel, sliding to a stop. Raider looked all around. No signs of hired guns. Maybe the straggler had been the only one to skip the explosive dinner in the bunkhouse.

"McPeters!"

Raider waited for the rotund land speculator to come out of the hotel. The plan was for him to look in the back and see the dead figure of Clanton. When he was shocked enough, Raider would draw down on him. Nice and clean. A good plan.

171

But it never came off the way the big man had figured it.

He heard something that had ruined more than one of his smooth schemes.

A woman screamed.

Raider's black eyes bulged. "Helen!"

She screamed again.

Raider unraveled his hands and came down off the wagon seat.

"No!" Benedict cried.

But Raider kept going. He crashed through the hotel door, running through the lobby to Adrian Thornton's bedroom. She screamed as he put his Justin boot to the lock. He drew down on Alexander McPeters, who was dressed only in his long johns.

McPeters gaped at the big man. "You!"

Raider grabbed the man's neck and put the pistol barrel between his eyes. "You hurt her, you son of a bitch?"

Helen stood against the wall, quivering, with her shoulders bare. McPeters had ripped her dress. He had also added a shiner to the mark left by Ace Clanton.

Helen nodded. "I'm okay, Raider. Don't kill him."

Raider started dragging him out of the hotel. "He's not gonna sleep here," the big man said. "He's gonna spend the night in the livery, chained to an anvil. Then I'm takin' him back to Phoenix for trial."

He rushed him through the lobby, out into the street.

McPeters stumbled on the sidewalk and fell into the dust, almost crashing into a coach wheel.

"There he is, Benedict. How'd you ever get into business with a man like him? Hell, you ought to be more careful. A man has to be choosy when he's pickin' a partner."

A rifle lever chortled above him. "Good advice, big man. Drop it."

Raider wheeled around, staring up at the second floor.

The bartender held a Winchester on him.

"That ain't very smart, barkeep," Raider said, his hand frozen by his side. "You better think it over."

"I have," the bartender replied. "Remember what I said about a man havin' to look out for his ownself? And now you're talkin' about choosin' a business partner. I chose Mr. McPeters here. He's payin' me top dollar to guard him.''

McPeters scrambled to his feet. "That's right."

"Drop the iron, Raider. We might even let you live." The barkeeper had the angle. "Mr. McPeters, get his gun."

McPeters slowly lifted the Colt from the big man's holster.

"Don't shoot him!" Helen cried from the hotel door. "I'll do whatever you want, Mr. McPeters. Just don't kill Raider."

The fat man swung the Colt around, thumbing back the hammer. "No, my dear, I'm going to kill *you*." He aimed right at her.

Raider flinched when the shot went off. But Helen was still standing, her eyes closed in terror. McPeters buckled instead, staggering forward with a dazed look on his face. Raider saw the hole in the back of his head as he fell.

The pistol fire had come from the roof of the general store. Raider looked back to see a hooded figure standing behind the parapet. A smoking gun in the cowled man's hand.

"You in the window," said the Spanish voice. "Drop it."

But the Winchester rang out in the morning air. The man on the roof tensed, holding his chest. He fired off a single burst and fell to the street below.

Raider dived for his own Colt, which had fallen out of McPeter's hand. He came up firing at the second-story window. The bartender cried out and fell through the casement, leaning halfway down the wall, hanging there with blood dripping from the hole between his eyes.

Helen Mallory ran across the street to the hooded man. "It's the padre. He's hurt."

Raider was right behind her.

He leaned over the man and pulled the cowl away from his face. "Not the padre," he said. "Just a soldier. The padre's brother."

Diego Pedroza quivered with a weird smile on his face. "When did you know, sēnor?"

Raider shrugged. "I put a few things together. When you dressed up like your brother, you wore a gold cross instead of a wooden one. You had a good chance to take one of his robes. And when I realized it was Clanton who tried to kill me, I figured you were the one who was fightin' for the sodbusters.

You knew how to shoot, and you weren't afraid to fight, the way your brother was.''

Diego gasped for air. "My brother is a good man, Sẽnor Raider. He does not fear fighting, only killing. I am ashamed that I masqueraded in his image. Please tell him the truth.''

"I know the truth already, my brother.''

Father Pedroza came out of the alley beside the general store.

"Goodbye, Amerigo," Diego said, coughing blood.

Raider looked down at the wound in his gut. "Hang on, Diego. I might be able to take that bullet out of you.''

"No, sẽnor. I want my brother to give me the last rights. I want him to forgive me.'' Diego held out his hand. "Brother?''

Father Pedroza knelt, taking his brother's hand, administering the last rites.

When Diego closed his eyes for the last time, the bizarre smile stayed on his lips.

The padre was crying. "I believe he found peace at the end.''

"Let's bury him," Raider said. "I'll dig the grave. I'll be proud to dig the goddamn grave. Oh, sorry, padre.''

Pedroza had not even heard him. "We'll bury him at the base of the mountains," the padre said. "He always liked it out there.''

"We'll bury 'em all out there," Raider replied. "Except for McPeters. Like it or not, I got to take his body back to Phoenix. If I don't, I'll catch all kinds of hell from ever'body.''

The padre nodded.

They used the coach as a funeral hearse. Helen went along, but the Benedict brothers stayed behind. Raider did not hold it against them. They had been through a lot for city boys.

When Clanton, Thornton, the henchman, the bartender, and Diego were in the ground, Raider turned with the shovel, peering toward the mountains.

Helen moved next to him, putting a hand on his shoulder. "What are you looking at?''

Raider exhaled. "I saw somethin' back in those hills. The Mescalero took me there. It's a funny thing to think about now that everything is over. I ought to be thinkin' about them people in the ground, but this is on my mind.''

"What?'' Helen pleaded. "Tell me.''

"Gold," the padre replied.

He looked up from his Good Book.

Raider eyed the hooded preacher. "You see it too when you brought me out of that pass half-dead?"

The padre reached into his robe. "I saw this." He tossed a big chunk of something at Raider.

The big man caught the piece of rock.

"That is all you saw," the padre said. "You saw a lie because of the drink the Mescalero gave you."

Raider held up the shiny hunk of ore that glittered in the sunlight.

"Gold!" Helen exclaimed.

Raider shook his head. "Fool's gold. Any tenderfoot can see that."

Pedroza smiled faintly. "I knew you would think of it sooner or later. So, I took that chunk for you, so you would know that you had missed nothing."

Helen sighed. "It sure looks real."

"God does not favor rich men," Pedroza offered. "Blessed are the meek, for they shall inherit the earth."

Raider looked at the chunk of fool's gold, thinking that they sometimes inherited the ground—six feet under.

Raider heaved the rock toward the mountains.

He stared at the sunbaked peaks. "El Dorado," he said softly.

Helen looked at him. "What?"

"Nothin', honey. Not a goddamn thing."

He blushed. "Sorry, padre."

Father Pedroza said something that sounded like a blessing.

CHAPTER NINETEEN

There was a lot for Raider to do when he got back to town. He had to wrap up the body of Alexander McPeters and get it under some straw. The corpse could ride in the rear of the coach when they went back to Phoenix. Raider did not anticipate any trouble with the authorities, as he had three solid witnesses. McPeters would be buried as an outlaw.

The Benedict brothers were receptive to Raider's idea of everybody leaving Adobe Sands in the coach. Both of them wanted to rest for a day, however. They also promised to make good with the homesteaders by offering them a chance to come back until the railroad people bought the land, or to take double the price again for their acreage. Raider thought that sounded fair.

They vowed to testify before the territorial marshal, claiming their innocence in all of McPeter's and Clanton's wrongdoings. If it took every penny they had, they were going to see that justice was served. Raider assured them that the marshal would dismiss the whole thing when he heard the truth.

Raider left them in Adrian Thornton's old office.

He needed a drink.

He moved out into the street, heading for the livery. After he had checked on his stallion and on McPeters's body under the straw, he went across the street to the saloon. The whiskey was going to taste pretty good.

He found something extra behind the bar.

Helen looked up from a shot glass.

Raider laughed. "Looks like we had the same idea."

"Birds of a feather," she replied with a tired smile. "Belly up, cowboy. You want hot whiskey or warm beer?"

Raider took off his Stetson. "How about both?"

He strode toward the bar, keeping his eyes on her pouty face. She felt bad. Why not? Everything under her had collapsed in less than twenty-four hours. It hadn't been that good before then.

Raider lifted her chin. "Hey. I want to thank you."

She looked away, pouring him a slug of red-eye. "Thank me for what?"

He shrugged his shoulders. "Well, for one, you stayed out of my way toward the end there. You coulda weaseled me out to Thornton."

Her face grew serious. She put her hand on his forearm. "Raider, I was scared. Clanton started bullying Adrian. I thought he was going to come after me. He wanted to be in charge."

Raider put his hat on the bar. "Thorny had some bad luck. If he had been a little smarter . . ." He lifted the shot to his mouth and drank it.

Helen scoffed. "If Adrian had been a little smarter, he wouldn't have been with me."

Raider dropped the glass on the wooden surface. "Hey, now, honey, don't go runnin' yourself down. Hell, you're about as loyal as any girl can be."

She raised an eyebrow. "Really?"

"Sure," he replied. "You were ready to do anything to save me. You told that to old McPeters."

She lowered her head. "I wasn't sure what you would think of that. I didn't know what I was saying."

Raider put his hand on her shoulder. "Well, you sure did right by me. I mean, most people woulda been tryin' to save their own tails."

Helen poured him another drink. "Loyal," she said, frowning. "That isn't much."

Raider's tongue was warmed by the second drink. "Hey, you're pretty, too."

She smiled reluctantly. "Really?"

"I ain't seen many prettier," he replied. "If I was to see

you on the street in Phoenix, I'd think you were a fine lady, one of them women who has breedin' and good blood.''

She laughed, but a tear started down her cheek. ''Thanks, Raider. You're bein' sweet. But why don't you just face the truth? I have. I'm at the end of the trail. There's no place else for me to go.''

Raider slammed his hand on the bar. ''That's where you're wrong, Helen. I done checked with the brothers there, and they said you can ride back to Phoenix in the coach.''

Helen shook her head. ''There's nothin' for me in Phoenix. If I'm gonna go, I'd rather head further east. Maybe New Orleans or Atlanta.'' She looked into Raider's black eyes. ''Maybe you could come with me.''

Raider exhaled, grimacing. ''Honey, I work for a man that sends me all over Creation, lookin' for them that's done wrong. I ain't never been west of Little Rock in my whole born days.''

She bit her lip, looking down. ''I didn't think you'd want to come.''

He poured a third shot and threw it back. ''Tell you what, honey. I'll get you to Phoenix and spot you to enough money for the stage east and enough for a train ticket when you reach a railroad.''

Helen smiled, suddenly feeling much better. ''Hey, that's nice of you, Raider. Heck, I may even like Phoenix.''

They drank some more.

When half the bottle was gone, Helen began to laugh uncontrollably over nothing.

Raider joined her.

They finished the bottle, laughing intermittently.

Finally, Raider looked up at her, his smile slacking into a half-serious expression. ''Helen, I don't want you to think wrong of me, but I figure after ever'thing I can say it.''

Helen leaned on her hands, grinning. ''Go on, handsome.''

''Well, what say we find a quiet place and cuddle up?''

She wrinkled her nose. ''Okay.''

''Bartender said he had a place upstairs.''

Helen took his hand. ''Yeah, a straw mat on a wooden floor.''

Raider frowned. ''But the Benedicts are on the ground floor at the hotel. They'll hear us if we—''

She put a finger to his lips. "Shh. It's a damned hotel. I know a place in the back where they won't hear us if we scream our lungs out."

He kissed her lightly on the lips. "You're a smart woman, Helen. I think you're gonna do just fine."

They hurried to the back entrance of the hotel.

Helen stopped in the bathhouse, insisting that they take a long bath before they went upstairs. She locked the door and they got undressed. When the wooden tub was full, they climbed in, soaping, rubbing, feeling.

"Now," Raider said.

"Not until we rinse."

She poured buckets of cold water over his head, but his ardor was not lessened.

Helen wrapped a towel around her and ran up the back stairs.

Raider chased after her without a towel.

He caught her in a bedroom on the second floor.

Helen fell back on the mattress, her large breasts falling to both sides.

Raider slid down next to her.

"I want it, cowboy," she whispered. "And I always get what I want."

As he slipped into her, he figured she sure as hell did.

EPILOGUE

On a bright Monday morning in Chicago, Titus Tilden sat at his desk, his eyes flickering toward the front door every few minutes. If the messenger didn't show up before noon, Tilden planned to dispatch another Pinkerton agent to find Raider. Tilden had reached the end of his patience. There had been no word for almost a month.

He opened a book on his desk. Stokes was available. He had found the train robber sitting down to supper with his family. The man hadn't caused any trouble, had even invited Stokes in for a meal. Raider did not like to work with Stokes, but then again, the big man from Arkansas did not like to work with anyone.

The front door swung open. Tilden peered out onto Fifth Avenue for an instant. The messenger closed the door behind him and turned toward Tilden's desk. He held up a letter that had come in the afternoon post. He had just gotten it from the mailman.

Tilden thanked the lad and dismissed him.

He looked down at the dirty envelope. Raider's scribbled handwriting in the address: "Mr. Allan Pinkerton, Fifth Avenew, Chicago, Illinoyse." And below, in a postscript: "or Titeass Tilden."

Tilden ignored the spelling and tore open the report. It had obviously not been written by Raider. A woman's hand had penned the three paragraphs on the faded parchment.

"I'm Helen Mallory," it read, "a friend of Raider's."

Titus would have bet on their being more than friends. The

woman had obviously been educated. She was quite eloquent in a rough way. At least someone had taught her to read and write—a cut above Raider's usual choice of women.

He continued reading. "I'm writing this while we are waiting for the stage. See, Raider came looking for the padre, only he found out the padre wasn't causing no trouble. It was somebody who dressed up to look like him. And he was protecting the sodbusters anyway so there wasn't any harm done."

Tilden stiffened. No trouble indeed. The cryptic nature of the message implied that a few bodies had been scattered around.

New paragraph. "Anyways, Raider found out that a man named Clanton and a man named Alexander McPeters had been [a misspelling of harrassing crossed out] bothering all of them. What was done against them was done in need. The territory law has been told about this and they are in agreement."

That made Tilden breathe a little easier. Although he planned to make inquiries in Arizona. Raider would probably get another commendation. That galled Tilden.

He braced himself for the salutation. "The main matter is that the killing has stopped. And the homesteaders have been offered a chance to come back. Those who would come back would be loco unless they just wanted to wait for the railroad, which caused the trouble to begin with.

"Written by Miss Helen Mallory for Raider with him telling me what to say outright."

Raider had put his name below hers.

Tilden read the report again. It made sense. He could read between the lines enough to add the report to his foreknowledge of the case. As usual, Raider had gotten results.

The report was still a strike against him. His nerve—letting one of his paramours write an official agency document. What would Allan Pinkerton think about the unorthodox submission?

He saw the broad figure of Pinkerton striding across the office floor. Wagner was right beside the big Scotsman. Wagner lifted his finger and crooked it at Tilden.

Titus fell in beside them, entering Pinkerton's private room.

"I'm glad you called me in, sirs," Tilden started. "I'd like to show you something if you—''

Pinkerton shook his head. ''Not now, Titus. Something else has come up. We just received the telegram today.''

Tilden forgot the letter for a moment. Pinkerton handed him the wire message. Wagner cleaned his glasses while Tilden read it.

''An attempt on the governor's life?'' He looked up at his supervisors. ''When did this happen?''

''Yesterday,'' Pinkerton replied. ''But you'll not hear about it in the *Chronicle*. The California authorities want to keep it quiet.''

Tilden nodded. ''I can understand that.''

''They want us to help,'' Wagner rejoined. ''In case there are any subsequent attempts. They've requested eight men.''

Tilden smiled triumphantly. ''Seems we're getting quite a reputation.''

''We've had one for quite some time,'' Pinkerton replied with a stern look. ''Best to work hard and worry about your job. Fame doesn't mean a thing.''

Tilden took the cue, humbly listing their eight best agents. When he had finished, Pinkerton struck one name. ''Take Stokes off.''

''But, sir . . .''

''I want one spit-and-polish man available for the field,'' Pinkerton continued. ''Keep Stokes free.''

Tilden struck the name and then looked up. ''Who should I put on instead?''

''Raider,'' Pinkerton replied.

Tilden started to protest. ''For this delicate work we can't—''

Wagner touched his shoulder. Tilden turned toward him. Wagner only nodded. Tilden looked back at Pinkerton, but there was no recourse.

Tilden sighed and penciled Raider beside the number 8.

In a last-ditch attempt to besmirch Raider's name, Tilden offered the report that had been written for Raider by Helen Mallory. ''Before you send Raider to California, sir, perhaps you should read this dispatch that arrived today. I'm sure you'll find it interesting.''

Pinkerton leaned forward and took the dirty envelope. He did not take out the letter. Nor did Wagner show any interest in the report.

"Aren't you going to read it?" Tilden asked impatiently.

"Yes," Pinkerton replied, still making no effort to read the dispatch. "That will be all, Titus."

Tilden could do nothing but exit under Pinkerton's stern eye.

Wagner slipped on his spectacles. "You shouldn't dress him down like that, Allan. He works extremely hard."

Pinkerton sighed deeply. "I know, but sometimes I feel I have to keep him in line."

Wagner nodded at the dirty envelope. "If it's like Raider's usual reports you'll probably want to shoot him if you read it."

Pinkerton nodded. "No doubt."

"What are you going to do with it?" Wagner asked.

Pinkerton swung the envelope over the fire of an oil lamp on his desk, keeping it there until it burst into dull, yellow flames.

J.D. HARDIN

**"THE MOST EXCITING
WESTERN WRITER SINCE
LOUIS L'AMOUR"
—JAKE LOGAN**

_0-425-07700-4	CARNIVAL OF DEATH #33	$2.50
_0-425-08013-7	THE WYOMING SPECIAL #35	$2.50
_0-425-07257-6	SAN JUAN SHOOTOUT #37	$2.50
_0-425-07259-2	THE PECOS DOLLARS #38	$2.50
_0-425-07114-6	THE VENGEANCE VALLEY #39	$2.75
_0-425-07386-6	COLORADO SILVER QUEEN #44	$2.50
_0-425-07790-X	THE BUFFALO SOLDIER #45	$2.50
_0-425-07785-3	THE GREAT JEWEL ROBBERY #46	$2.50
_0-425-07789-6	THE COCHISE COUNTY WAR #47	$2.50
_0-425-07974-0	THE COLORADO STING #50	$2.50
_0-425-08088-9	THE CATTLETOWN WAR #52	$2.50
_0-425-08669-0	THE TINCUP RAILROAD WAR #55	$2.50
_0-425-07969-4	CARSON CITY COLT #56	$2.50
_0-425-08743-3	THE LONGEST MANHUNT #59	$2.50
_0-425-08774-3	THE NORTHLAND MARAUDERS #60	$2.50
_0-425-08792-1	BLOOD IN THE BIG HATCHETS #61	$2.50
_0-425-09089-2	THE GENTLEMAN BRAWLER #62	$2.50
_0-425-09112-0	MURDER ON THE RAILS #63	$2.50
_0-425-09300-X	IRON TRAIL TO DEATH #64	$2.50
_0-425-09213-5	THE FORT WORTH CATTLE MYSTERY #65	$2.50
_0-425-09343-3	THE ALAMO TREASURE #66	$2.50
_0-425-09396-4	BREWER'S WAR #67	$2.50
_0-425-09480-4	THE SWINDLER'S TRAIL #68	$2.50
_0-425-09568-1	THE BLACK HILLS SHOWDOWN #69	$2.50
_0-425-09648-3	SAVAGE REVENGE #70	$2.50
_0-425-09713-7	TRAIN RIDE TO HELL #71	$2.50
_0-425-09784-6	THUNDER MOUNTAIN MASSACRE #72	$2.50
_0-425-09895-8	HELL ON THE POWDER RIVER #73	$2.75